A Journey in

Purity

A Theological Novel

Richard P. Belcher

Crowne Publications, Inc.
P.O. Box 688
Southbridge, Massachusetts 01550

Printed in the United States of America

ISBN 0-925703-39-7

AUTHOR'S PREFACE

Our first theological novel, *Journey in Grace*, has been so well received, that it has been even a greater delight in preparing this second effort. Several questions must be answered, which we did not address in the first book.

First, the events in these books are not auto-biographical. Though every author writes out of his own knowledge and experience, such writings are not necessarily depicting the exact events of his own life.

Second, the events of these books, especially the present one, is not the experience of any one pastor I have known.

Actually, both books are the product of the writer's almost four decades of experience in not only pastoring and preaching in local churches, but of talking with numerous pastor friends, and from counseling dozens of his former students now serving in churches scattered throughout the United States.

Thus this is the story of dozens of men of God, with the events in places changed and rearranged and edited for the production of the story.

If some of the events sound almost beyond belief--that is, such things could not happen to a pastor in this twentieth century in the United States--be assured that these events (and much more) have been shared with the author, many times through burdened and puzzled hearts.

This book is dedicated to all those pastors who have travelled or who are now travelling a similar journey in purity, as they have sought to preach the truth in a local congregation, whereby they might bring that church back to accountability and responsibility in this undisciplined age.

Contents

CHAPTER 1

WHAT SHALL I DO WITH THE SLEEPING GIANT?

*And why call you me, Lord, Lord,
and do not the things which I say?*
Luke 6:46

I could never have anticipated, even in the wildest dreams of an active imagination, the blessings which had become mine in the winter of 1972. Nor could I have anticipated the pain which was to follow in that next year!

The blessings were many. For one thing, I was pastor of a fairly prestigious church, the First Baptist Church of Collegetown, even though I was only a senior in college myself. They had called me as pastor from the Lime Creek Baptist Church, a rural church, after I had spent a year there as a student-pastor. I had done all I could to discourage them, but the small faithful remnant of about fifty to sixty who attended out of a membership of around a thousand had insisted I was the man to lead them. When God finally convinced me of that fact also, I accepted the invitation to be their pastor.

Another blessing was that I had been married to Terry Lynn Lasitor that Christmas season of 1971. Following our honeymoon we had settled into the parsonage to serve the church, and I was also determined to finish my college degree and then go on to seminary.

Another blessing was that I was settled theologically. Terry and I had pursued the basic doctrinal issues the previous year before our marriage, coming to the conclusion we were in agreement with the doctrines of grace.[1] My plans for the future not only included schooling and pastoral work, but I hoped very soon to enter upon a study of the subject of eschatology--the doctrine of last things.

I must confess that there was a matter or two about the church I pastored which troubled me. The greatest concern was our gigantic number of inactive members. We did have fifty to sixty who attended regularly, but we also had about nine hundred plus who never attended, or at best attended only occasionally. Yet, like most Baptist churches of our denomination, the Evangelistic Baptist Convention, they were still considered full-fledged members with all membership privileges, including voting rights.

I had sought to contact all of the church members the first few months of my pastorate, and had discovered several things in the process. First, several hundred of them couldn't even be located--they were not only inactive, but they were also non-resident. Many of these were even non-traceable--we couldn't find an address for them. Yet their names were still on our church roll!

A second thing I discovered was that many of these inactive members who were resident gave no evidence of any concern to live a holy life or in getting back into church. Their weeks and week-ends were spent in pleasure and self-seeking. They had no interest in Christ or His church or in a preacher who was concerned about them. Some were even rude to me when I called on them. Shockingly though, when I suggested to several of them they might want to find another church or withdraw from our church until such time as their lives and interests gave evidence of spiritual concern, they acted as if they were insulted at such a suggestion. They informed me that they were church members and they were willing to fight to keep that privilege, though they had no intention of changing their lives or life-styles.

To be honest these people scared me. I had already seen several hundred of them mobilize to try to keep me from moving into the parsonage after I had accepted the call of the church.[2] They had been stirred up by Dr. Bloom and only Mrs. Bloom's intervention had dispersed them. Yet I realized they were a time-bomb ticking constantly while waiting for some issue to set them off in an explosion.

I had inquired also as to how and when these people had been received into the membership of the church. I discovered that some had united as children simply because that was what was expected of them. When you reached a certain age, you made your "profession of faith" and were baptized and joined the church. Others, I found, had united as a result of some sensational and high-pressured evangelistic meetings and practices which had been prevalent during the fifties and sixties. They had made professions also, and maybe had attended for a little while, and then dropped out never to show much interest or concern thereafter.

I wrestled giving serious thought as to what I should do with this sleeping giant, but I had to confess, I knew of no way to deal with them without tearing the church apart. Perhaps I needed a little time to further establish myself and my ministry before attempting anything.

Little did I realize during those early days of 1972 that in God's providence I would face the issue very soon, and in a way that would bring unimaginable pain to myself and Terry and the faithful fifty of the church who supported me.

If I could have had my way I would have let the giant sleep a little longer before I faced him, but that was not the plan of my sovereign Father.

---

[1] See Richard P. Belcher, *A Journey in Grace* (Southbridge, Massachusetts: Crowne Publications, 1990).

[2] Ibid., pp. 93-95.

...it is better, if it must be so, to stand, like a marble statue, on the pathway of obedience, than to reach the most desirable ends by transgressing a plain precept of the Word of God.

---C. H. Mackintosh

To be left unmolested by Satan, is no evidence of blessing.

---Author Unknown

CHAPTER 2

WHO WANTS TO START THE THIRD WORLD WAR?

The cup which my Father hath given me,
shall I not drink it?
John 18:11

The battle for church purity began, even though I was not ready for it nor did I initiate it, on a Monday morning as I was in my office at the church. I had attended an early class at school, and was working on Sunday sermons when I received a phone call from Conrad Spratt, the chairman of my deacons.

"I thought you might like to know that Miss Lilly was in a car wreck this morning and is in the hospital," he informed me.

Miss Lilly was one of our fairly regular attenders. She appeared to be a very sweet and generous soul. In my single days as a pastor there, she had kept me in regular supply of cookies, cakes and pies. She had even brought a whole meal a time or two. To say the least, I was concerned at this news of her accident for I had considered her to be one of the most spiritual members I had.

"How is she?" I asked.

"Oh, she's alright," Conrad assured me.

I gave a sigh of relief as he paused. Then he floored me with his next statement.

"There's something you should know," he declared rather matter of factly. "She was given a ticket at the scene of the accident for DUI."

"A ticket for DUI?" I shouted in unbelief. "Are you telling me that Miss Lilly was driving under the influence of alcohol--really? There must be some mistake. Not Miss Lilly!"

I could not believe it. Tell me that Clark Kent isn't Superman, or that the Lone Ranger shot Tonto, or that Roy Rogers never had a horse named Trigger, but don't tell me

Miss Lilly was driving drunk! Not Miss Lilly!--the sweetest, kindest, most humble and most thoughtful little woman in our church. It could never be!

Then Conrad floored me again as he said, "Oh, that's nothing new. She's had a drinking problem for years."

He then proceeded to tell me that the last person to ever know of her problem is the pastor. She saves her kindest actions for him. In fact, the last pastor, he informed me, used to take her each week to the doctor, he thought. He would wait in the parking lot of the medical building while Miss Lilly was in the doctor's office. The only thing was that though she entered the doctor's office, she didn't stay there. She would slip out the front door, walk across the street to the liquor store and buy her bottle or two for the week. She would then slip back into the doctor's office, sit for awhile, and then go back out to the parking lot so the pastor could take her home. He never knew the truth--that he was giving her transportation to buy her booze each week.

He continued, "I guess she was driving today because she had not gotten around for some reason to ask you to transport her. Only somewhere between the liquor store and home she stopped at someone's house and they drank for a spell before she tried to continue home."

When I asked why someone had not told the pastor, if everyone knew of it, he was rather silent. When I asked why someone hadn't confronted Miss Lilly with her problem, he replied, "I guess the answer to both those questions is that no one wanted to start the Third World War."

I asked him what he meant by that.

"Well, Miss Lilly is pretty close to a lot of the inactive members of the church--in fact she's related to a lot of them. If anyone were to make an issue of her problem, they would all rise up in her defense. It's easier to ignore the matter and go on in peace."

As I hung up the phone, I knew something had to be done--I could not ignore the matter. Something had to be done for Miss Lilly's sake. Something had to be done for the church's sake. Something had to be done for the community's sake. Surely Miss Lilly would not be averse to my offering to help her in her physical and spiritual need. She had always expressed great appreciation for my sermons and challenges to the church.

I started for the hospital, rehearsing what I would say. I reminded myself that Miss Lilly's condition was my chief concern. I was quite confident that she would admit her problem and be open to my offer to help her. After all, she was a friend, I thought--one of the sweetest and most humble persons I had ever known.

How wrong I was! I really didn't want to, but I was soon to see the start of that Third World War!

When nothing whereon to lean remains,
When strongholds crumble to dust;
When nothing is sure but that God still reigns,
That is just the time to trust.

'Tis better to walk by faith than sight,
In this path of yours and mine;
And the pitch-black night,
When there's no outer light
Is the time for faith to shine.

---Author Unknown

CHAPTER 3

WILL THE REAL MISS LILLY PLEASE STAND UP?

When thou passest through the waters,
I will be with thee...
Isaiah 43:2

I left my office and headed for the hospital immediately. I was still planning my strategy when I walked through the front door. I didn't feel any need to take someone with me-- not to see Miss Lilly. I did ask myself if there was a possibility that I really didn't know the real Miss Lilly. She would have been the last person I would have thought could have a drinking problem, let alone deceive her pastor to take her to the liquor store weekly. But then I assured myself that I could handle the matter alone.

When I entered her room, she greeted me with her usual warmth and friendly smile as if nothing was amiss. Maybe she hoped I hadn't heard of the DUI charge, or that if she was kind enough to me, I wouldn't mention it.

"Oh, my dear pastor, I'm so sorry to make you come out to the hospital to visit me," she offered before I could speak. "You really didn't need to come. I'll be going home soon. It was only a minor accident."

After assuring her of our love and prayer for her, and after discussing the details of the accident for several moments (she made no mention of her intoxication), I tried to approach her problem very delicately.

"Miss Lilly, no one has been kinder to me since I have been pastor here than you," I spoke for openers.

She beamed with pride, and I continued.

"And, Miss Lilly, there's no one in our church that I love more than I do you. You have been something of a mother figure to me."

She beamed again and muttered something about the blessing I had been to her. I continued cautiously searching for words.

"Miss Lilly, I don't know how to mention this, but it has come to my attention that you may have a problem that you need help with and I want you to know that because I love you, I want to help you."

I could never have anticipated what took place next. She became an entirely different person. Immediately she turned cold and unfriendly. The sweet, gracious, warm and friendly Miss Lilly was gone, and in her place was a monster.

"What problem?" she barked at me.

"Miss Lilly--please! I'm not here to condemn you. I want to help you. Please let me! Your problem is common knowledge in the community and in the church, and now the accident has brought it out into the open. When I say I want to help you, please believe me that I have your best interest at heart."

That did it! She now spoke with a cold hatred and rejection.

"Preacher, I don't need your sermons this morning. I've gotten along all these years without some inexperienced young know-it-all preacher trying to run my life. I don't need your help spiritually or physically. You'd better leave this hospital room, or you'll be sorry--I'll see to that."

How shocked I was! This was not the same Miss Lilly I had known. What was going on here? Had she been playing the part of the hypocrite all these months I had known her? Foolishly, I tried again.

"Please, Miss Lilly, I only want to help you in your relationship and walk with the Lord, and in any problem which might hinder that walk."

She replied now with a vengeance.

"Listen, you young squirt! When I stand before God, I have no doubt my good deeds will outweigh my bad deeds, and on that basis I have no doubt I will get into heaven. Don't you remember all those cakes and cookies you took from me? So I sin in some ways. Who doesn't? Do you want to tell me that you're perfect, preacher? Now get out of my hospital room!"

I started to speak, but it was obvious that she was not going to allow that.

"I think it's obvious that God accepts me. He spared me in this wreck, didn't He? And if it wasn't for my faith, I don't know what I would do."

How could I reason with that kind of twisted logic? She wanted to excuse sin on the basis that no one is perfect. She mistook God's kindness in sparing her as an evidence of salvation. And she had no respect for me at all. What a conglomeration of confusion.

I decided at this point that it might be best to leave as she had suggested. She was so mad that I almost expected steam to come out of her ears.

As I was turning to go, two of her elderly friends walked through the door. I recognized them as two of my inactive members. They and all their families were members, but they never darkened the door of the church.

As soon as Miss Lilly saw them, she burst into tears. I have never seen a change come upon one so quickly. She went from hatred and rage to her sweet humble act. She began to sob her heart out as if she were crushed.

Of course her friends rushed to her side to comfort her.

"Oh, you poor thing!" they both declared with a sympathy which showed Miss Lilly's act was accomplishing its purpose.

"What's wrong, Lilly?" they asked over and over again. But she didn't answer at first, obviously seeking to build tension and greater interest in her plight. Then she faked a try several times.

Finally she spoke, but the lie that came out of her mouth was a beauty--pure falsehood.

"Girls, the pastor just told me I was going to hell if I didn't repent and get right with God! Girls, am I really as bad as that--that God would send me to hell?"

Again, at the end of the statement the crocodile tears flowed, and her friends smothered her with the sought-for sympathy. They also both looked at me with utter disdain, obviously again one of Miss Lilly's goals in her hypocrisy.

Then one of her friends spoke siding with her.

"Well, that's what we get for calling such a young and inexperienced pastor. Young man, anyone ought to know you should never insult a person and tell them they are going to hell, especially one in the hospital who has just had an automobile accident. Besides, everyone knows what a fine Christian Miss Lilly is. Doesn't the Bible tell us not to judge lest we be judged? Brother Park, our former pastor, would never have done anything like this. He was a perfect gentleman. You can be assured that the church will hear of this."

It was obvious that these ladies would never believe what I had just witnessed in the Miss Lilly metamorphosis. In fact, if I hadn't been there during our conversation, I might have believed Miss Lilly's version of the events also. Her performance was that convincing.

I left clearly shaken and deeply troubled over the possible repercussions this could bring to the church and my ministry. Must a pastor always live in uncertainty of the future? One person can lie about you and your ministry is destroyed either in that place or perhaps for the entire future. What a life of insecurity! And how could I ever hope to defend myself?

As I drove back to the church (I sensed the need of more time in prayer), I saw that the matter touched the area of my deepest concern at the church--the impure membership problem. If God did not intervene, the sleeping giant would rise and throw me out.

I was quite depressed when I reached the church. I didn't think matters could possibly get worse, but very soon they did!

CHAPTER 4

SHOULD I RESIGN
THE CHURCH?

...we must through much tribulation
enter into the kingdom of God.
Acts 14::23

As I drove to my office I mulled over in my confused mind what exactly had just taken place. Had I been insensitive in word or action to Miss Lilly? Had I handled the matter correctly? Exactly what was the conversation which had taken place between us?

I asked these questions for several reasons. First, it was essential that I establish the unfolding of events because of the accusations which these ladies, especially Miss Lilly, would bring against me. But more than that, if I had been wrong in my handling of the situation, I wanted to know it so I could make it right. Nothing I could have done would have justified how Miss Lilly acted, but still I was responsible for my actions just as she was for hers.

I made the following notes to summarize the hospital visit:

1. Miss Lilly had greeted me very cordially and had thanked me for coming to visit her--so far so good.

2. I then assured her several times and in several ways of our love and prayer for her in this hour.

3. I then discussed the details of the accident with her but made no mention of her intoxication.

4. Then I tried to approach her with her problem, but re-affirming to her that I spoke to her of the matter only because of my love for her. I did not accuse her of being lost, at this point, nor of being destined for hell.

5. It was then that she not only denied the problem, but she also became very cold and rude toward me. She turned argumentative and ordered me our of her room.

6. When her friends walked into the room she went back to the sweet personality of Miss Lilly and began to cry to gain the sympathy of her friends.

7. It was then that she accused me of telling her that she was going to hell if she didn't get right with God. But I had not used the word hell, nor had I even hinted that she was lost. At first I had told her I was concerned about her relationship and walk with the Lord. I must confess, as the encounter continued she gave evidence doctrinally and practically that she may well not be a Christian, but she never gave me an opportunity to get that far in our conversation. Even if I had used the terms repentance and hell there was no ground on her part for being offended, because my attitude was proper and Christ-like.

8. It was out of her false accusation that her friends also upbraided me with further statements of false accusation and disrespect.

Having made these notations, I read back over them before typing them to be sure of their accuracy. I was convinced that this was an accurate account and summary of our conversation.

Next I stated some clear questions with answers following:

1. Had I been insensitive to Miss Lilly? NO.

2. Had I told her she was going to hell? NO.

3. Had I handled the situation with grace and love? YES.

4. Would I do anything differently were I to do it over again? YES.

5. What? I would take someone with me as a witness to establish the conversation. As it stood now it was Miss Lilly and her friends' word against mine.

I was sure at this point that the sleeping giant would believe Miss Lilly and her friends, but what of the 50 or 60 regular attenders who were so insistent on my coming to pastor. Would they stand with me in any problem that might arise? And if they would, what was 50 against hundreds?

It seemed my whole ministry, present and future, stood before me as if it were hanging by a thread on the edge of a cliff ready to topple over were someone to give it a slight push. I was certain the sleeping giant, when he came alive, would have sufficient strength to destroy me and my ministry at First Baptist Church of Collegetown.

Why not beat them to the punch and resign before the explosion? Why not give myself full-time to my schooling? Maybe the Lord could open another door like Lime Creek Baptist Church, my first pastorate--a place where people loved and appreciated my ministry.

Was the coming battle worth it? Was it worth the damage it would leave in its wake? Damage to the church! Damage to my reputation! Damage to my future ministry and opportunities to pastor!

No one but the faithful fifty had felt it was God's will for me to come as pastor anyway. When I had accepted the church, critics abounded even among my fellow pastors and other workers and leaders in the denomination. Some had openly stated that the church was making a serious mistake when they called me. I was too young and inexperienced. I was lacking in a full education. I lacked maturity, they said.

So now why not be humble about it and admit we had made a mistake? That surely would be easier to recover from than the mess I saw coming. Some would even congratulate me and herald my wisdom and maturity for admitting that I had gotten in over my head.

As I read the Word of God and prayed (mostly complaining and questioning prayer), I could not remember a time in my life when I had ever felt more alone and defeated.

Where was God in this battle? Why had He allowed it to happen? Why didn't He stop me from accepting this church? Why hadn't I seen this inevitable clash in light of the sleeping giant I knew had existed?

Various passages did bring some comfort.

> *Blessed are they who are persecuted for*
> *   righteousness sake; for theirs is the kingdom of*
> *   heaven.*
> *Blessed are ye, when men persecute you, and shall*
> *   say all manner of evil against you falsely, for my*
> *   sake.*
> *Rejoice, and be exceedingly glad; for great is your*
> *   reward in heaven; for so persecuted they the*
> *   prophets who were before you.*
> *   Matthew 6:10-12*

Right now on earth I found it rather hard to rejoice and be glad, let alone EXCEEDINGLY GLAD. What did reward in heaven mean to me right now, when I was facing such hardship on earth?

I could not imagine things getting worse, but very soon, believe it or not, they did!

CHAPTER 5

COULD THIS POSSIBLY BE FROM THE LORD?

And it came to pass after awhile, that the brook dried up,
because there was no rain in the land.
I Kings 17:7

I didn't leave the church that evening until about 5:30. By then it was dark, being January. I had called Terry and shared the events of the day with her.

After locking the church door, I was walking the few yards to my car when all of a sudden, two hooded men stepped out from behind the bushes. They had some instruments in their hands which appeared to be heavy wooden rods, but I couldn't really tell in the dark. Whatever they were, they began to swing them at me.

I dodged several swipes, but with two of them firing at me I soon caught one which sent me sprawling to the ground. Immediately my hands and arms covered my head for protection of my face and skull area, and I kept rolling and twisting on the ground to make myself a difficult target. Even so, their blows found the target and kept landing on various parts of my body.

Two thoughts went through my mind.

"Who are these guys and what are they trying to do to me--kill me?"

Finally, though I don't know how, I was able to get to my feet. But instead of running, I lowered my shoulder and charged one of my attackers reminiscent of my high school football days when I had played some defense and tackled a ball-carrier. This put both sticks out of action, since the one I tackled could not hit me at such close quarters, and the other would not try for fear he might hit his partner as we rolled on the ground.

In the struggle which followed I did the only thing I thought would discourage them--I grabbed the hood of my opponent and pulled it off. I recognized him as one of my inactive church members--the son of one of the ladies who had visited Miss Lilly in the hospital room.

Exposed to the world he grabbed his hood and shouted to his friend, "Let's get out of here!"

They ran around the corner, I heard an engine start, and they sped away.

I didn't have the energy to chase them. I remained on the ground gasping for air as I was exhausted and spent from the exertion of the struggle. I suddenly was aware that each breath and gasp for air shot pain through my chest and back areas. I became conscious of blood on my face and hands.

Finally I struggled to the car, and after fumbling with the keys to unlock the door, I collapsed into the front seat with my feet outside on the ground. Every movement was painful, but I finally pulled my feet into the vehicle and searched for the ignition with my hands and for the pedals with my feet.

As I drove home I marvelled that I had been able to ward off my attackers.

But then I wondered, "What kind of people are these? How far will they go to get their way? Don't they have any Christian principles that govern their lives?"

After a short drive which seemed like three times the distance, I pulled into the driveway and honked the horn. Terry came out wondering what could possibly be wrong. When she opened the passenger side of the car and the dome light came on and she saw me, she screamed. She insisted that we go immediately to the hospital. She offered to drive, but to be honest, I didn't know if I could manipulate my body from the driver's seat to another place in the car, so I drove.

On the way to the hospital through my moans and groans I told her of the attack. Now she was furious! She offered to pray as I drove, and did she ever pray! She prayed for me, for my attackers, for the whole situation and ministry at First Baptist Church and for God to be glorified in the whole situation. I could tell by the tone of her voice that she was hurting as much as I was.

The hospital kept me, and after the usual entrance requirements, I finally settled into what I knew was a soft bed, but it wasn't very soft that night. Terry left me for about forty-five minutes to go home and get some things, so I was alone for awhile.

As I sat staring into the darkness of the room, I broke and began to cry. I was hurt physically, emotionally, mentally, and spiritually as never before in my life.

I concluded as I wallowed in my sorrow and self-pity that this little episode had settled it.

Surely the Lord would not require his servant to go through more of this.

Surely there is a nice quiet place where I could labor without such problems.

I concluded I would resign at the next public service of the First Baptist Church of Collegetown. Who wants or needs more of this? Not me!

I was so shaken and skiddish that I almost expected someone to step out of the darkness of the room and hit me again, but no one did.

I was glad when Terry got back. I would tell her of my decision tomorrow. Under some sedation I drifted off into dreamland--nightmares of men coming at me out of the darkness with sticks.

Is the midnight closing round you?
Are the shadows dark and long?
Ask him to come close beside you
And He'll give you a new sweet song.
He'll give it and sing it with you;
And when weakness lets it down,
He'll take up the broken cadence,
And blend it with His own.

And many a rapturous minstrel
Among those sons of light,
Will say of His sweetest music
'I learned it in the night.'
And many a rolling anthem,
That fills the Father's home,
Sobbed out its first rehearsal,
In the shade of a darkened room.

---Author Unknown

CHAPTER 6

HOW CAN I PROVE MY INNOCENCE?

...we were pressed out of measure, above strength,
insomuch that we despaired even of life;
but we had the sentence of death in ourselves,
that we should not trust in ourselves
but in God, who raiseth the dead...
II Corinthians 1:8-9

I woke up the next morning in more pain than the night before. This brought with it a greater determination to resign. I could hardly wait till the next service to read them my statement of resignation. Maybe I would even send it to be read by the chairman of the deacons if I was not able to attend for a while. My mind began to form the wording of that statement.

Then I became aware that Terry was sitting quietly in the chair in the hospital room and she was reading her Bible. I wondered how I would ever share my decision with her, when she spoke.

"The Lord has been showing me some tremendous verses. Let me share some of them with you."

To be honest I was so spiritually and mentally low that I didn't want to hear the Bible, yet I understand now that such a time is when one needs to hear the Word the most.

With a quivering and broken voice which evidenced what she had gone through during the night in the searching of heart, she read the following:

If it had not been the Lord who was on our side, now
*   may Israel say,*
If it had not been the Lord who was on our side, when
*   men rose up against us;*
Then they had swallowed us up quick, when their wrath
*   was kindled against us;*

Then the waters had overwhelmed us, the stream had
*   gone over our soul;*
Then the proud waters had gone over our soul.
Blessed be the Lord, who hath not given us as a prey to
*   their teeth.*
Our soul is escaped like a bird out of the snare of the
*   fowlers; the snare is broken, and we are escaped.*
Our help is in the name of the Lord, who made heaven
*   and earth.*
                  Psalm 124:1-8

I had to admit that it was an appropriate section of
Scripture. Several parts of it ministered to my soul.

"If it had not been for the Lord who was on our side..."
They might have killed me!

"Our soul is escaped..." It could have been much
worse. Though I am stretched out on a hospital bed, it
could have been much worse.

"Our help is in the name of the Lord...." Had He not
helped me the previous evening? Would He not stand by
us and help us in the future?

She continued to read several others, which also revived
my soul and began to change my outlook.

I will say of the Lord, He is my refuge and my fortress;
He is my God. I will trust in Him
                  Psalm 91:2

The Lord is on my side. I will not fear what can man
do unto me.
                  Psalm 118:6

The Lord is my light and my salvation; whom shall I
fear? The Lord is the strength of my life; of whom shall
I be afraid?
                  Psalm 27:1

Then she read several portions from Psalm 57.

*Be merciful unto me, O God; for man would swallow
me up; he, fighting daily, oppresseth me. Mine enemies
would daily swallow me up; for they are many that fight
against me, O thou Most High. What time I am afraid, I
will trust in thee. In God I have put my trust; I will not
fear what flesh can do unto me. (1-4)*

*Every day they wrest my words; all their thoughts are
against me for evil. They gather themselves together,
they hide themselves, they mark my steps, when they
wait for my soul. (5-6)*

*When I cry unto thee, then shall mine enemies turn back:
this I know; for God is for me. (9)*

*In God I have put my trust; I will not be afraid what
man can do unto me. (10)*

*For thou hast delivered my soul from death. Wilt thou
not deliver my feet from falling, that I may walk before
God in the light of the living? (13)*

I marvelled as we went back over that psalm--it seemed
to have been written just for me.

My enemies would fight against me and swallow me up.
    They fight against me daily.
    They wrest my words.
    They have continual thoughts against me.
    They hide themselves.
    They mark my steps.
    They wait for my soul.

But I have put my trust in my God.
    I will not fear what flesh can do to me.
    I know my God is for me.
    I cry to Him and my enemies are turned back.
    I will not fear what man can do to me.

I have been delivered from death.
I will be delivered from falling.
I will walk before God in the light of the living.

To say the least, my soul was lifted from reading and meditating on this section of Scripture. My thoughts of resigning didn't make much sense or sound very spiritual anymore. I didn't even mention them to Terry.

Who was I to think I could follow my Lord without suffering when all the saints before had walked in that pathway?

Who was I to desire an easy life when the very heart of my faith was a cross upon which my Savior had suffered and given His all for me?

A familiar hymn began to float through my mind:

> Am I a soldier of the cross,
> A follower of the Lamb?
> And shall I fear to own His cause,
> Or blush to speak His name?
>
> Must I be carried to the skies
> On flowery beds of ease,
> While others fought to win the prize,
> And sailed through bloody seas?
>
> Are there no foes for me to face?
> Must I not stem the flood?
> Is this vile world a friend to grace,
> To help me on to God?
>
> Sure I must fight, if I would reign;
> Increase my courage, Lord;
> I'll bear the toil, endure the pain,
> Supported by Thy word.

I had to admit the easy path, which is what the flesh craves, would be the desirable action. But how could that possibly be God's will?

Was He not a sovereign God?

Had He not in His sovereignty led me here?

Was He not sovereign over all these events--even Miss Lilly's accident and actions in the hospital?

Was He not sovereign even over the men who had beaten me? They could not have lifted a finger against me without His allowance or will.

Was He not doing something in my life and the life of the church which needed to be done?

Would He not sustain me? How I did not know--but was that not the heart of a life of faith?--we follow Him not knowing where or what but trusting Him whatever comes.

Then something struck me. I realized there was not one hint of resignation thinking in Terry's mind. She spoke in words of faith as she had taken her refuge in the Word.

Again, I had to marvel at her spiritual life and wondered how many preachers' wives discourage their husbands in the ministry even in the best of times, let alone in the times of difficulty and persecution. I remembered several of my friends at school who were fighting that battle right now--an uncooperative wife or a wife without faith to face the tests and trials of the ministry.

I rested during those early morning hours, before they started the tests, rejoicing in the Lord. Then as the day passed under the scrutiny of the hospital machines and doctors and nurses, I began to wonder what I would do next. Several questions faced me immediately.

Should I prosecute the men who had attacked me?

How could I stop the flow of misinformation and falsehood which I knew was now running rampant throughout the community and church family?

But the biggest question was, how could I ever bring purity to this church of 1000 members with only 50 or so of the members backing me and giving any evidence of a godly mind and spiritual desires? Anything I thought of doing to try to bring godliness and purity to the church would tear the church apart, so it seemed.

Late in the afternoon, when I had returned from all the tests, I had two other visitors--a couple of young policemen who stopped by to take a report of my assault. I gave them a full account and even identified one of my attackers. When the report was finished and they were getting ready to leave, one of them shocked me with a rather blunt statement.

"Look, preacher! I may only be a policeman and may make no profession of religion, and I don't know what they teach you out at that Baptist college, but it seems only common sense to me that you made a real mistake when you walked into this hospital and told Miss Lilly that she was going to die and go to hell if she didn't repent of her sins. I know Miss Lilly has some problems, but you just played right into her hands when you said what you did."

I shocked him in return by asking, "Officer, what's your name?"

He stammered a few seconds, perhaps thinking this mean old preacher, who had so devastated Miss Lilly was going to cut loose on him."

"I, uh, uh, meant to be helpful. I'm sorry if I offended you."

Maybe he also thought I was planning to report him to his superior for he was still reluctant to give me his name. Sensing his uneasiness, I assured him I was not offended by his remark and had no intention of making trouble for him. Really, I was more interested in learning who had told him of my encounter with Miss Lilly.

Finally he spit out his name.

"I'm Troy Medford!"

I realized instantly that he had the same last name as the attacker I had recognized and identified.

"Are you any relation to Alan Medford, one of my attackers?" I asked him.

He blushed as he admitted they were cousins.

"Great!" I thought to myself. "I have a policeman investigating my case who is related to one of my assailants and who believes Miss Lilly's false accusations. What chance did I have of justice?"

Then I realized that such a thought might be equally unjust to him as the accusations I faced were to me.

I addressed him again.

"Officer Medford! When you make an arrest and no one is present except you and the criminal, and you handle the case exactly according to the book, and then the criminal accuses you of police brutality or some other injustice against him, how do you defend yourself?--especially when you are innocent but everyone else believes the criminal and thinks you are guilty?"

He got my point as he stated in a puzzled way, "You're telling me you are innocent? You're telling me that you didn't tell Miss Lilly that she was going to hell if she didn't repent of her sins?"

"Yes, but how do I prove it?" I asked him.

He had no answer to that question, but he seemed touched as he realized my problem--one he might face in police work. As he left I assumed I might never see him again, although under other circumstances he might have been a good evangelistic contact.

The question remained--how can I prove my innocence?

The answer came also. You cannot! God must be your defender!

Be still my soul: the Lord is on thy side.
Bear patiently the cross of grief or pain;
Leave to thy God to order and provide;
In every change He faithful will remain.

Be still my soul: thy best, thy heavenly Friend,
Thro' thorny ways leads to a joyful end.

---Katharina von Schlegel

CHAPTER 7

ARE YOU REALLY
AN
EVANGELISTIC BAPTIST?

*And seekest thou great things for thyself? Seek them not;
for behold, I will bring evil upon all flesh, saith the Lord,
but thy life will I give unto thee for a prey in all places
to which thou goest.
Jeremiah 45:5*

My wounds, so they told me, were not serious--only painful. I think I could have told them that. Battered hands, bruised shoulders and legs, and some painful but unbroken ribs were the extent of my damage. They decided to keep me at least one more day to run some further tests just to be sure of no internal injuries.

I encouraged Terry to go home for the evening and rest, but she refused to do so. Then in the course of the next few hours several visitors entered the room, though to be honest, I would have preferred to have been left alone.

The first visitor was the associational director of missions of our Evangelistic Baptist denomination. He was the overseer of the work of Baptist churches in our county. In reality he possessed no authority over the churches or over me as a pastor, though I am not sure all the people in the churches understood that clearly.

He greeted me and we exchanged pleasantries for a few moments before he sat me on my ear with what he had come to say.

"Several members of your church came to see me last night. They're very concerned about the course of your ministry there at First Baptist Church."

Questions began to jam my mind demanding to be spoken, but I started with an obvious one.

"Who were these 'several members' who visited you?" I asked.

"Well, they asked me not to identify them, though they did give me the freedom to tell you of their visit if I thought it might be helpful."

He left the door open, so I stepped in.

"Does it not raise some question as to what kind of people these are who hide their identity but not their dissatisfaction? Is that not the action of cowards?"

"Now don't get uptight about it," he said with a calmness. "They may have felt there was the need for someone to mediate for them with you."

"Then you have come as a mediator?" I asked.

"Well, if I can help, I am always available," he countered.

"Were they deacons?" I continued.

"No," he admitted.

"Were they other church leaders?" I asked continuing to press him.

"Well, not that I know of," he admitted again.

"Do they attend regularly?" I probed further for more information.

"Some may and some may not," he answered elusively.

I concluded that either he knew and didn't want to admit their lack of attendance or he didn't know and was hiding the fact that he had not even established who these people were and had listened to non-attending and unspiritual people. He had been conned by the sleeping giant.

"What is their concern about the course of my ministry?" I continued.

He stuttered and stammered for a few seconds, and then finally got the words out.

"Well, they're upset about the Miss Lilly thing, but they had questions about you even before that episode. They're not convinced that you're a true Evangelistic Baptist."

"Oh?" I asked playing it coy. "And what reasons did they give for these doubts?"

"Well, you're not like the previous pastors," he remarked gaining confidence now.

"And what is the difference?" I challenged.

"You don't preach like their previous pastors. You preach through Bible books and always address believers about living a holy life instead of addressing the lost each service. They said they had loved ones who need to make their profession of faith and join the church who never will as long as you're there because you don't give them opportunity to do so. This worries them--to think that you stand in the way of their loved ones' salvation."

I smiled as he spoke. They wanted me to preach evangelistically every Sunday? They didn't want any expository preaching through the various Biblical books? They think the salvation of their loved ones is dependent on the evangelistic preaching of the preacher every Sunday and their walking down a church aisle and joining the church?

He wasn't finished.

"They say you don't have an invitation hymn every service. You don't plead with the lost to come forward after every sermon to make their public confession of faith so they can be saved. And when you do have a closing hymn you call it a hymn of worship and invitation and only sing a few verses instead of really pleading with the lost to come forward for salvation."

I thought to myself that they were hung up on some form of "decisional regeneration." God can only save a person as he or she comes forward in the church.

But again, he wasn't finished.

"Also, you don't observe all the denominationally suggested Sundays. You just keep preaching through Biblical books. Also you have had other speakers in the church besides men of our denomination. So there is a real question of your loyalty to the denomination."

I had always thought the denomination existed to help a church or pastor as it or he desired, but now they and this director of missions seemed to be advocating that the local church and pastor exists to do the bidding of the denomination. Failure to do so was seen as disloyal. What had happened to the authority and autonomy of the local church?

And again, he wasn't finished.

"Plus, some of them are afraid you might try to remove their names or the names of some of their family members from the church membership," he spoke almost chiding me.

He explained further, "After all, it's not the practice of Evangelistic Baptists to remove names from the membership roll. Rather, we must love every member and work with them, and try to get them back into the active life of the church."

I listened and finally he got to the Miss Lilly issue.

"And, of course, you can understand they are also concerned with your clash with Miss Lilly. They're convinced you should never have said what you did to her, and now, having said it, you should be quick to apologize. If you don't, they think you should resign."

I was interested to see if he believed the Miss Lilly accusation. He had stated the matter as something of a fact, not even asking me of the truth or falsity of it.

"And what if the Miss Lilly accusation were utterly false, and is being used as a point of contention by a group of unspiritual people to seek to defeat the work of God in First Baptist Church?" I asked him forcefully.

"Well, I think there may be some misunderstanding between you and Miss Lilly as to what really happened. She may have misunderstood you and you may have misunderstood her as well. Probably it is the case of where both of you acted wrongly. Whatever, you should be Christian enough to be willing to apologize and admit the thing got out of hand--that you never intended to say whatever it was you said. If it will smooth the matter over and save your ministry there, what does it matter? The main thing is the promotion of unity and harmony in the church."

"And what if I am not willing to admit your analysis of the matter, but that it is a clash between truth and error, and that the purity of the truth is more important at times than unity, and that there cannot be a true unity based on falsehood and compromise?" I asked, looking at him only out of the corner of my eye.

"Then I think that you ought to resign as pastor and let them call someone in who will bring unity!" he stated firmly. "After all, there are others churches in our denomination which you can pastor. You don't have to be here. And if you stay and this thing becomes a mess, you may ruin your career with Evangelistic Baptists forever."

"I see you speak with determination," I observed.

"Well," he replied, "there are some things which cannot be compromised."

"I'm glad you agree," I stated. "The only thing is that we disagree on what cannot be compromised. But we both agree there are some things which cannot be compromised."

I think I lost him on that one. He looked puzzled, so I continued.

"You want me to compromise the truth for the sake of a purity and unity based on error and falsehood. To you denominational loyalty is more important than truth. To you pleasing unfaithful church members is more important than the truth. When I refuse to compromise my convictions for your false convictions in these areas, you get very determined and demand that I compromise my convictions. Yet you won't compromise your conviction about my conviction even though it may bring a disunity between us. Therefore, you have sacrificed your principle of unity and peace at any price which you are trying to press upon me."

I'm not sure he ever understood what I had said to him. He did leave and Terry and I were left standing in utter amazement.

"Can you believe that," I stated with a fury. "Here is a denominational leader meddling in the affairs of a local church without invitation from the leadership--the pastor or the deacons or the church by a vote."

"And did you get the accusations against you?" Terry took up. She then rattled off a list of accusations as if she had sat taking notes on our conversation.

"You're not a true Evangelistic Baptist because you're not like the previous pastors. Where does Scripture come in here as the guide concerning what a pastor should be?

"Also, your preaching is questionable because you preach the Bible! Isn't that what a preacher is supposed to do?

"You don't have long invitations at the end of your sermon. You don't brow-beat people to come forward and make a profession of faith.

"You don't observe denominational days. Where is the local church's autonomy here? You bring in speakers outside the denomination. Maybe that's because so few of the denominational men can preach.

"You're going to remove their names from the church roll. But why do they want to be members if they do not wish to attend and support the church?

"You should apologize to Miss Lilly. Nothing like a pronouncement of guilt before a fair trial or hearing. He didn't even ask you what you said.

"And you should resign for the good of the church and the future state of your career and ministry."

I took it up from there.

"Yes, I guess according to him Elijah should have apologized to the prophets of Baal. Jeremiah should apologize to the people of Jerusalem. Paul should apologize to the Judiazers. Martin Luther should apologize to the Roman Catholic church. Jesus should apologize to the scribes and Pharisees."

"Yes," she added, "and God should apologize to Satan."

The point was, and perhaps we were overstating it in our frustration, that truth and error have always been in conflict, and there is not only the conflict of the two, but the price to pay as one stands for the truth against all error and falsehood.

As I turned on my bed, I was reminded of that fact in real and painful terms.

CHAPTER 8

WHERE DO WE GO
FROM HERE?

*He who dwelleth in the secret place of the Most High
shall abide under the shadow of the Almighty.
Psalms 91:1*

As I dozed after the visit of the director of missions, I came to see clearly what needed and had to be done. The church needed to be purified. Years of false evangelistic practices had dumped multitudes of questionable professors into the membership of the church. Many of these probably were not even saved. Yet they wanted to continue to have a part in the life and decisions of the church even though they had no intention of attending.

Even if they were Christians, they were untaught, being fed only a diet of shallow evangelistic sermons, if they attended the church services at all.

My heart was encouraged greatly by another visitor about an hour later. It was Conrad Spratt, the chairman of my deacons. He was the first one I had spoken with who showed any evidence of understanding the situation correctly.

"Don't worry, pastor," he said immediately. "The fifty or sixty faithful attenders are standing with you."

That was good news to me, but I wondered what these few could do against hundreds, except the Lord intervene for us.

"We met last night in two groups in homes for prayer," he continued. "We organized to pray faithfully daily until the Lord has His way in this matter."

"I guess you all have heard the accusations Miss Lilly has made against me?" I asked.

He smiled and laughed and then apologized for his laughter as he spoke.

"Forgive me for laughing, Pastor. Yes, we know Miss Lilly is lying about you. So does everyone else--even the trouble-makers. But they wouldn't admit it because the lie gives them an issue with which to attack you and to get the sympathy of the uninformed. And they are milking it for all it's worth. But we are confident that somewhere along the line the Lord will expose Miss Lilly's lies. We don't know how or when, but He will."

I sat amazed at his depth of spirituality and faith. He was a sincere and spiritual man to begin with, and he also had grown immensely under the Word just the past few months.

I shared with him my concern and even asked for his input on the next step.

"Where do we go from here?" I inquired.

"Well, I think it might be helpful if you make a general statement to the congregation about not believing every accusation they might hear about you. Second, I think you need to address the deacons. I believe they're all solid behind you, but the enemy will work on them and pressure them to work against you. Beyond these general suggestions, you're better at the details than I am."

After we had prayed and he had left, I began to count my blessings. What a change had taken place in the last twenty-four hours. I had gone from utter discouragement and a desire to resign my church to rejoicing. I had also been given a desire to stay and trust the Lord to sustain me.

Besides the change in attitude, I had a wife who was standing with me. I had a group of people who loved me and who were uniting behind me also.

I knew the road ahead would be rough, and that now I did not have all the answers. But I knew He would go with me and be true to His promises. I said with Paul in this hour:

> *We are troubled on every side, yet not distressed; we are*
> *perplexed, but not in despair; persecuted, but not*
> *forsaken; cast down, but not destroyed;*
> *Always bearing about in the body the dying of the Lord*
> *Jesus, that the life also of Jesus might be made*
> *manifest in our body.*

> *For we who live are always delivered unto death for*
> *Jesus' sake, that the life also of Jesus might be made*
> *manifest in our mortal flesh.*
> *II Corinthians 4:8-11*

A sermon outline from this passage began to form in my mind as I meditated in that section of Scripture.

I   <u>What We Are As Christians</u>
     we are troubled on every side
     we are perplexed
     we are persecuted
     we are cast down
     we are bearing in our bodies the death of the Lord Jesus
        Christ

II   <u>What We Are Not As Christians</u>
     we are not distressed
     we are not in despair
     we are not forsaken
     we are not destroyed

III   <u>Why We Are What We Are As Christians</u>
     so that the life of Jesus might be manifested in our body
     so that the life of Jesus might be manifested in our mortal
        flesh

No doubt about it! Wherever the Lord would lead us in the future, whatever we would have to suffer, He would not forsake us. However fierce the battle, it would result in the Lord Jesus being manifested in our bodies--in our mortal flesh. What could be better than that!

THE CONQUEROR

No matter how the storms may rage
Upon the sea of life,
No matter how the waves may beat,
No matter what the strife;
The Lord is just the same today
As when He walked the Sea,
And He can conquer every storm
That life may send to thee.

The waves are raging everywhere
And men are sore distressed,
But all they need is found in him
Who giveth perfect rest;
So cast your care upon the Lord,
Whose strength will never fail;
He calms the waves for your frail bark,
His power will e're prevail.

---Selected

CHAPTER 9

YOU HAVE PROOF OF MY INNOCENCE?

He turned the sea into dry land;
they went through the flood on foot;
there did we rejoice in him.
Psalms 66:6

The hospital kept me one more evening and then released me on a Wednesday. I was still sore and bruised, and even walking was painful, but I was determined to attend the prayer meeting of the church that night. I had decided this would be the time to make the general statement.

The service itself was uneventful, except for a slightly larger crowd, which included some of the trouble-makers. Neither Miss Lilly nor her two friends nor my attackers were present. The faithful fifty were very loving and sympathetic, which did give me a confidence and a sense of support.

Finally the time came in the service for me to make my statement. I read it as follows:

During the term of a pastor's ministry, you may hear many statements and accusations against him. One of the easiest things to do is to make a false accusation against someone, and the enemy does seek to bring such accusations against the servants of God in the ministry especially. Many are eager to hear and believe such lies, and care not for proof of guilt in the matter. If someone says it, they believe it.

I hope you will realize that to make such a false accusation against a man of God is a serious matter and such an individual will give an account to God for that action. But also, please realize it is a serious matter to believe and spread such a false accusation, and the one guilty at this point will be held accountable by God also. Remember, too, that the Lord in His time will deal with both the accuser who makes the lie and the accomplice who spreads the lie in Satan's attempts to discredit God and His servant.

I trust you will remember these facts, especially in these days when recently false accusations have been brought against me as your pastor. In time I am confident the full truth will be brought forward with proof, but until then, please believe me and trust me. If you have further questions about this statement and the accusations which have been made, please feel free to contact me or one of our deacons for further counsel and explanation.

When the service was over, I tarried at the main door to be available for any feedback or question which might come regarding my statement. Most everyone was strongly supportive. A few appeared to have slipped out another door rather than face me.

Finally the building was cleared and Terry and I headed for our car. As I closed the church door behind me, I remembered the last time I had taken this walk, when I had suddenly been confronted by my two attackers.

I was somewhat apprehensive when I noticed the blackness of the darkness. Then my heart fell and I was stopped in my tracks when I saw a figure standing in the darkness beside the same bushes from which I had been attacked.

In one motion I pushed Terry behind me, handed her the keys to the building and told her to go get help. I was ready, even though my body still ached with pain, to stand between any attacker and Terry, not only to protect her but also to give her an opportunity to get inside the church and call for assistance. She was hesitating, not wanting to leave me alone in my condition, then a voice spoke up.

"Preacher Pointer? I don't mean to scare you, but I have to talk to you. And I didn't want any of the people to see me."

"Who is it?" I barked demanding to know the identify of the figure addressing me.

"It's Troy Medford. Do you remember me? Officer Troy Medford. I visited you in the hospital room and took the report of your attack."

"Are you alone?" I asked, wondering if he had brought some of his family with him.

"Yes, I am alone. Can I talk to you a few minutes?" he asked.

I had no idea what he had in mind, and at this time of night especially. But we went back into the church to my office, taking care to lock the doors behind us, and with Terry present as a witness with his agreement (I wasn't too sure of this Medford family), he began to unravel a strange but interesting story.

"I'm in trouble, " he said, "and you may be the only one in this town who can identify with me and understand what I am going through at this time. Have you seen today's paper?" he asked.

I had to admit that though I was a regular reader of the daily paper, the events of these past two days had kept me from that normal practice.

"Well," he continued, "if you had read the paper today, you would know that I shot a man while on duty last night. The victim and several of his friends were burglarizing a local store, and when we arrived and confronted them, a struggle evolved, he drew a gun on me, and I had no other choice but to shoot him. He died a few hours later at the hospital."

He broke down and began to cry.

I sought to console him.

"Well, you had no choice, did you? He faced you with a gun--what were you supposed to do?"

"Yes," he agreed, "it was self-defense," he continued as he spoke through more tears. "But I can't prove it!"

"Why not?" I asked somewhat puzzled. "If he pulled a gun on you, they surely have it as evidence and such evidence will validate your claim."

"That's the strange thing," he informed me. "No gun was found at the scene of the crime. When I fired, all his friends with him in the robbery scattered, and in the confusion one of them must have taken the gun with him.

They were all caught later, but no gun was found with them or on them. Now they are saying that they were all unarmed, including the boy I shot, and that I shot him without provocation."

"Well, what about your partner?" I queried.

"In the struggle that preceded the shooting, he was knocked out and now he doesn't know a thing about the shooting because he was unconscious. So you see, preacher, you and I are in the same boat. We are accused of some action that we cannot prove we did not do."

His answer made it clear we were both accused, but did he believe I was innocent as he also claimed to be?

"Are you saying that you believe I am innocent also?" I asked.

"Preacher, I not only believe you are innocent, but I know you are and I can prove it!"

To say the least, I was shocked and asked him to explain the proof he had found in my behalf.

What followed was proof beyond dispute of my innocence. But these words were not the greatest words I heard that evening. Far greater were the words he spoke to the heavenly Father as a sinner crying out for salvation as he acknowledged his sin and surrender to the saving power and Lordship of Jesus Christ. This commitment came after we had talked several hours, and after I was sure he understood the gospel and its requirements. It was not a shallow or surface decision, as far as I could tell, but a serious and knowledgeable one.

I also shared with him how I had prayed and had been trusting the Lord to come to my aid in unearthing evidence of my innocence. I urged him to do the same.

I asked him to keep the proof of my innocence to himself until I was ready to use it at God's appointed time. He agreed, we prayed together, and then walked out to the car. I must admit I felt more comfortable making that walk with a policeman by my side.

As Terry and I drove home, it was a time of rejoicing. How quickly God had come to our aid! He had not only vindicated his servant, but he had given us a precious soul in the process. Praise the Lord.

And some were accusing me of not being a true Evangelistic Baptist!

Now I had to figure out the best time to unveil the evidence of my innocence. I hoped such an unveiling would have a calming effect on the storm that was brewing, but I couldn't be sure that would be the case.

On the way home Terry and I sang.

> Jesus, Lover of my soul,
> Let me to Thy bosom fly,
> While the nearer waters roll,
> While the tempest still is high!
> Hide me, O my Saviour hide,
> Till the storm of life is past;
> Safe into the haven guide,
> O receive my soul at last.
>
> Other refuge have I none;
> Hangs my helpless soul on Thee;
> Leave, O leave me not alone,
> Still support and comfort me:
> All my trust on Thee is stayed,
> All my help from Thee I bring;
> Cover my defenseless head
> With the shadow of Thy wing.
>
> Charles Wesley

PEACE! IT IS I!

Fierce was the wild billow,
    Dark was the night;
Oars labored heavily;
    Foam glimmered white.
Trembled the mariners,
    Peril was nigh;
Then said the Saviour God
    'Peace! It is I.'

Ridge of the mountain wave,
    Lower thy crest.
Wail of the stormy wind,
    Be thou at rest.
Peril there none can be;
    Sorrow must fly
Where said the Light of Life
    "Peace It is I.'

      ---Selected

CHAPTER 10

WILL YOU DEACONS STAND
WITH ME?

*And there arose a great storm of wind,
and the waves beat into the ship, so that it was now full...
And he arose, and rebuked the wind,
and said unto the sea, Peace be still.
And the wind ceased, and there was a great calm.
Mark 4:37, 39*

The next evening was our regularly scheduled deacons meeting, and I had decided now was the time to begin working with them concerning the problem of impurity in the church. The chairman, Conrad Spratt, had contacted each one to be sure they would be present. I wasn't exactly certain then where these men stood concerning the false accusations against me, though Conrad assured me they stood with me. Five of them had been present the previous evening at prayer meeting and had expressed support.

Conrad moderated over the usual business, and then gave me the remaining time to address them. I began cautiously.

"Men, you will remember that it was a difficult decision for me when you called me and wanted me to be your pastor. I agonized over the matter for many weeks. I was deeply impressed and encouraged by the love and commitment of those attending, and especially your desire to build a spiritual church. But one thing concerned and frightened me more than anything else--the large number of inactive members on the church roll. I realized that group was a sleeping giant capable of rising to oppose any spiritual growth and progress God would give to the church."

I paused and was encouraged as I observed several of them nodding their heads in agreement. I continued.

"This sleeping giant showed itself, you'll remember, when I tried to move into the parsonage, as they were stirred up by Dr. Bloom. But the Lord stood by us and intervened in our behalf and defused the situation."

Again, I was encouraged as they listened intently in obvious agreement and not just with a blank bored stare. I continued.

"Now the sleeping giant is aroused again. I had hoped I could be pastor for several months and that we could map a Biblical strategy together to face this potential problem. But it is clear that our sovereign God had other plans. Through the Miss Lilly matter, the giant is rallying and thundering against us. It behooves us to be prepared and to act Biblically to solve or at least face the problem. If we do not, it may very well be the end of the spiritual life and power and witness of this church. But realize also, that even if we do act Biblically, we have no idea what the outcome may be. No doubt a spiritual battle will ensue, and remember that Satan and his forces play by no rules. We will see reactions and attitudes we never dreamed possible out of some who profess to know Him. We will hear unbelievable false accusations against us that many nonetheless will believe. We may be shocked in our own hearts as to what the enemy will do and we will also be embarrassed before the world as they will many times side with our opponents. Not only will we hear lies, but we will be assaulted with vile and ungodly attitudes."

I paused again to see if they were still with me. The nodding heads had stopped. A sober and serious attitude and atmosphere pervaded the room. I continued.

"Families may be split against families--children against parents and parents against children; brothers against sisters and sisters against brothers. The pressure to give in just to have peace could be unbearable. If we do not walk close to our Lord in the fray and battle and fight by the spiritual weapons of prayer and faith, and if we are not committed to do what the Word of God teaches over the feelings and sentiments of men, we will be crushed. Better not to take up the battle, if we are not determined to see it through in a spiritual manner, whatever the cost to us and our families. A Christian in his own strength is no match for Satan and his methods. He will eat us alive--unless we live and walk and fight by God's power and Spirit."

At this point I felt somewhat like a coach challenging his team before the big game or at half-time, but I knew the stakes were much higher than the winning or losing of some sports event--even the Super Bowl. The stakes were eternal!

I went on.

"There may be times when you will feel like quitting the battle. You may be tempted to resign the office of a deacon, or you may want to just leave the church and find some peace. You'll reason, 'This is not what I bargained for when I agreed to serve as a deacon.' If it will encourage you to know, I have already gone through those emotions and feelings. The night in the hospital, just following the beating, I was lower spiritually than ever before in my life. I even decided during that night, sometime in the wee hours of the morning, that I was going to resign and leave as your pastor. But God stopped me as He revived and renewed my heart the next day."

I noticed some astounded looks on their faces as I shared honestly my experiences of the past few days.

"I have no desire to continue this battle without your backing. God may have me do it, but it will be much better if we stand together. The easiest thing in the world would be for me to resign. My reputation is at stake. It may be ruined, humanly speaking, in this battle. My career, again humanly speaking, may be placed in jeopardy. Who wants to hire someone as a pastor who has had problems in his previous church? Already some are accusing me of not being a true Evangelistic Baptist. But I must admit, and I trust that you agree, there are some things more important than reputation or career or health or the future or even life itself, and that is faithfulness to God's Word."

At this point I felt I had to remove all doubt about the false accusations of Miss Lilly.

"Just in case anyone has any doubt of the accusations Miss Lilly is making against me, let me firmly deny them and assure you I have proof of my innocence, which information and evidence I will use as the Lord leads at the appropriate time. God has been so gracious in bringing this proof to me (I didn't even seek it), but please do not ask me to share with you what that evidence is because I will not regardless of the pressure you put upon me."

This confirmation of evidence brought several "Amens" and one "Praise the Lord!" I had several more points to make.

"Please understand that the major problem is not Miss Lilly or the clash with her. We could solve that and the problem would still remain. She is only a symptom of a much greater problem--an impure church. Our church is full of people who have made a profession of faith, but who give no evidence of salvation. They have no spiritual desires. They do not live godly lives. They attend at best only occasionally. They give almost nothing to the life and finances of the church. They never read or study the Word. They are unresponsive to attempts to encourage them to attend church and understand the responsibilities of church membership. Yet at the same time these unspiritual people have voting rights and stand ready to use that privilege against anything the faithful minority might wish to do."

Heads nodded in hearty agreement once again.

"What are we to do with these people that I call the sleeping giant? I cannot set before you a plan in one evening, because any plan we would formulate must be based on Scriptural foundations, and there is much more than just one Scriptural principle involved here. Here is what I propose--that we as a group meet every Thursday evening for the next several months and let me share with you what the Scripture teaches in relation to church purity and church discipline. We will take the subject step by step so that there will be no question that when I do suggest a final plan that we will all be agreed that we are acting on a Scriptural basis and therefore with God's authority."

Heads nodded again in solid agreement.

"In the meantime we must allow our Lord to work. The sleeping giant may try some maneuvers to oust us or to thwart us. But we must trust in our Lord's providence to sustain us until such a time as we are ready to act. Maybe in the process our God will give us converts out of the sleeping giant. Maybe He will act powerfully in His own way against members of that group as they would seek to destroy us. I do not know, but we must walk by faith. However impossible the situation may seem to become, we must walk knowing that many times in a spiritual battle that the darkest hour comes just before the dawn. We must remember that sometimes God allows a situation to deteriorate to hopelessness so that when the victory comes we will give Him the glory and not take it unto ourselves."

I paused here before facing them with the final question.

"Are you with me? Will you stand with me? Will you risk your reputation, your businesses, your future, your life, your all for the sake of the cause of Christ in this church? Jesus said that he who is not with Me is against Me, and the same is true here. There is no middle ground and there can be no straddling of the fence. The cause of Christ and His church is at stake. Will you deacons stand with me?"

They all agreed to my challenge and we spent another thirty minutes in prayer. It was a joyous time as I drove home, to know that God had given me those who would stand with me, but I was not foolish enough to think that just because of that the awakening giant would roll over and go back to sleep. And I would soon find out I was correct.

FAITH without works is dead.

---James 2:20

*FAITH and works are bound up in the same bundle. He that
obeys God trusts God; and he that trusts God obeys God.
He that is without faith is without works; and he that is
without works is without faith.*

---C. H. Spurgeon

*THEREFORE if any man be in Christ, he is a new creature;
old things are passed away; behold, all things are become
new.*

---II Corinthians 5:17

CHAPTER 11

CAN ONE BE
A CHURCH MEMBER
AND YET BE LOST?

For we are made partakers of Christ
if we hold the beginning of our confidence
steadfast unto the end.
Hebrews 3:14

In the days which followed it became obvious that the opposition was working cautiously behind the scenes. Several things happened to confirm that fact.

For one thing our crowd jumped the next Sunday from our usual fifty or sixty to ninety or more. Evidently, others of the group were too busy with their self-centered life-styles to attend, or maybe the issue was not hot enough for them yet. Of course all those new attenders were very sweet to my face and acted as if they were the strongest of my supporters. How deceitful men can be. Some of these, I found out, were those who had met with the director of missions. Soon, though, even these lost their interest and went back to their old ways of non-attendance.

For another thing, word came that they were meeting weekly on their own, evidently to plan strategy. Rumors began to scatter that they were circulating petitions for my resignation, an action I had expected would come.

Further, several of them had even expressed sorrow over the beating I had received. They told me to my face that they disagreed with me and felt I had been unfair to Miss Lilly, but that they wanted to separate themselves from the violent behavior of my attackers. I gave them the benefit of the doubt and accepted their statements as true and thanked them for their concern. I really wasn't too sure of their sincerety about the matter.

But harassment continued in other ways. One night an ambulance pulled up in our driveway in the middle of the night. It seems someone had called the hospital and said the pastor of First Baptist Church had been shot, and asked them to rush an ambulance to the scene. I guess the message they were sending was a threat of what could or would happen. I must admit that this frightened me somewhat, but I gave in to the hope that this action was that of a coward who would only bluff and not really carry out a threat. Obviously, the purpose of such an action was to scare me and maybe run me off. Perhaps someone thought I would break under such pressure and leave on my own.

Some positives did emerge that next week. Troy Medford and his wife were in church that next Sunday. Some were quite shocked and wondered why he was there. Maybe they assumed he was coming to back the opposition. I began to meet with him privately several times a week to disciple him, but had not encouraged him to make a public profession for a few weeks. He began to give in our meetings the evidence of a true conversion as he possessed a godly heart and spiritual desires. His interest in the Word of God was phenomenal.

His allegiance could not be hidden very long, because he began to witness to others in his family. They did their best to cause him to doubt what had happened to him, even though many of them professed to be Christians. It did show us that many of this group were not really concerned about the lost being saved, as they had claimed, but only of opposing my ministry.

Troy's problem on his job continued as the police department was still conducting its investigation of the false accusation made against him. We constantly made that situation a matter of prayer, and he seemed content that God would have His way whatever the outcome.

The next Thursday evening I met with my deacons once again. They were an interesting group. Eli Melton ran the local funeral parlor. Sam Booker was a local merchant and owned a clothing store. Ed Schuster was an insurance salesman. Bob Motley was a real estate broker. Bill Ashton was a doctor. Conrad Spratt, the chairman, was a lawyer.

I had wrestled extensively over the past few days as to where to begin to train my deacons in the necessity of a pure church. Many passages went through my head which I knew I would have to face eventually. But where does one begin?

I began with a question.

"Is everyone who claims to be saved really saved? Or to put it another way, is everyone who professes to be a Christian really a Christian? Or again, is every church member truly saved?"

They sat in silence, either unsure of an answer or unwilling to make a statement concerning it.

"Will you take the word of Jesus concerning this matter? If Jesus says it is possible to profess to be a Christian and not really be one, will we believe Him and side with Him and act from that conviction?"

I asked them to open their Bibles (I had insisted they bring one to our meeting) to Matthew 7:21-23.

I read the passage to them:

Not everyone that saith unto me, Lord, Lord, shall enter into the kingdom of heaven, but he that doeth the will of my Father, who is in heaven. Many will say to me in that day, Lord, Lord, have we not prophesied in thy name? And in thy name have cast out devils? And in thy name done many wonderful works? And then will I profess unto them, I never knew you; depart from me, ye that work iniquity.

I noted the following facts about these people spoken of by Jesus:

1. They called Jesus Lord.
2. They had prophesied in His name.
3. They had done many wonderful works in His name.
4. They had cast out devils in His name.

I challenged them to see the truth of this passage.

"Evidently from this foundation these people were convinced they were children of God. Probably others felt they were Christians also. Who would have doubted the reality of their profession of faith?"

I then asked them pointedly, "But what did Jesus say about them?"

With insight they offered the following:

1. Jesus said they will not enter the kingdom of
    heaven.
2. He said they never were saved--He never knew
    them.
3. He said they never did His will--their religion though
    done in His name was self-willed.
4. He said they are workers of iniquity even though
    they do religious works which appear to be
    Christian.
5. He said they shall be separated from Him for
    eternity.

I then quizzed them, "Are these individuals saved?"

They all shook their heads in the negative.

I repeated the question with some emphasis, saying, "These do not enter the kingdom of God. Are they saved?"

They answered, "No."

"Is it possible for one who never knew Christ to be saved?"

They answered again, "No."

"Is a profession alone enough to show that one is saved?"

They answered again with greater emphasis also, "No!"

"Is everyone who does church works saved?"

They spoke again in unison, "No!"

"Then we have agreed," I summarized, "that it is possible to be lost even though one professes to be saved; even though one has performed religious or Christian works; even though one claims to know Christ; and even though one has worked miracles in the name of Christ."

They all echoed, "Yes!"

I pressed them again.

"What is the true evidence of being a Christian?"

They looked at the passage a second, and then one of them said, "Doing the will of God."

"Then," I asked further, "should the one not doing the will of God claim to be saved?"

"Absolutely not!" affirmed Conrad Spratt.

We discussed these truths from our passage for awhile. Then I applied it to our situation.

"Could it be that the First Baptist Church of Collegetown has some members like this? They have made and continue to make professions that they know Christ. They have been baptized. They are members of the church. Some have and are doing what appears to be Christian works in His name. They would argue unrelentingly that they are truly saved. But they never were saved. They will not enter the kingdom. They are workers of iniquity. They shall be separated from Christ for eternity."

"The sleeping giant!" Dr. Ashton offered.

"The sleeping giant!" I echoed.

"Please be clear in your understanding," I warned. "We are not saying all of these inactive members are not saved. We can say that many of them give no evidence of salvation and we can place a large question mark on their profession of faith, even though they may have some religious works."

"But what shall we do with them?" Ed Schuster asked.

"That's a good question," I acknowledged. "The church should have been training and teaching them and holding them accountable through the years, but it has not. They are now like children who grew up without discipline and without accountability in a parent's home. It is much easier to train and discipline a child as it grows than to try to establish training and discipline after it has been neglected for a number of years. The same is true here. Since we have neglected training these professed converts and since we have not held them accountable, it will be very painful to establish accountability and discipline now."

I set before them a final question.

"Does the fact that there has been no accountability for years, and does the fact that the situation is extremely serious now, excuse us from doing something about it?"

Conrad spoke again.

"It seems to me that we have a great responsibility for people like this--to help them see their condition so they may see their need of Christ and salvation. If we are to be concerned about the lost, we must be concerned about these for such may clearly be lost and without Christ. To ignore them is to shirk our responsibility to teach and apply the Word of God correctly to all men in their need of spiritual help. The question is not, must we or must we not do something. The answer to that is indisputable, from my perspective. We must do something. The real question is, What should we do? What can we do at this late date after so many years of neglect?"

They all agreed with Conrad's conclusion, and so did I. I informed them that next Thursday night we would talk about what must be our next step.

At least now we were all agreed. One could be a church member and be lost, and the church had a responsibility toward such a person.

CHAPTER 12

HOW DOES ONE BECOME
AN UNSAVED CHURCH MEMBER ?

The sacrifices of God are a broken spirit;
a broken and a contrite heart, O God,
thou wilt not despise.
Psalms 51:17

My rejoicing and exuberance from the first meeting with the deacons carried over into the weekend. Not even a visit from one of the opposition to my office on Friday morning could dampen my spirits.

He was one of those who had gone with the group to complain to the director of missions. I found out later that he was even the leader of the band. On Friday he popped into my office. His name was Garth Duncan. He was the president of the local bank.

I welcomed him as best I could under the circumstances, wondering what his purpose was. It didn't take long for me to find out as he whipped out several pages of petitions from a briefcase and paraded them before me.

He declared confidently, "I have three hundred names of church members on these petitions calling for your resignation as pastor of this church. I think if you are wise you will see the hand-writing on the wall and go quietly on your own before we meet to vote you out."

I had to hand it to him. He was up front about the matter. He had come to see me face to face. He must be over-flowing with certainty of his strength in the battle to be so bold and open.

My next statement shocked him somewhat, and I wasn't sure he was going to stay after I insisted on certain procedures as we discussed the petitions.

I informed him that I was glad to discuss the matter with him, but only if my secretary were allowed to serve as a witness to establish the conversation. Understanding that I was serious and that his visit would result in nothing unless he agreed to my requirements, he finally agreed.

I asked him what grounds the petitions set forth as reasons for my resignation. His answer sounded like a repeat of the accusations his group had made to the director of missions. They questioned my loyalty to the Evangelistic Baptist Convention. They didn't like my preaching. I didn't give a long pressured invitation after every sermon. I wasn't evangelistic enough. I was having secret meetings with the deacons trying to brainwash them to my convictions. I was going to remove names in wholesale numbers from the church roll and place them on an inactive list taking away their voting rights.

On that last one he muttered something about my being a Communist because I was going to deny them their rights as Americans. I almost laughed at the theological and Biblical ignorance which stood before me, but I prayed the Lord would give me a love for him and help me in my reply to his list of accusations. I was glad my secretary was there to hear him call me a Communist. That may be worse than telling someone they are going to hell if they don't repent of their sins, I joked to myself.

When he was finished, I didn't even try to defend myself. I only asked him in a very friendly way to share with me his conversion experience.

He hesitated at first, but I asked him again, "Just share with me how long and when you were saved, and how it all took place. You are a Christian, aren't you?"

My question suggesting a possible doubt in my mind of his salvation was just the challenge needed to plunge him into sharing his supposed salvation experience.

"Well, preacher, I've always been a Christian. I have always loved the Lord and sought to obey the Ten Commandments. I joined the church making my profession during a revival forty years ago when I was ten years old. I've never strayed from him all these years. I've served as a Sunday School teacher, as a deacon, and in many other offices of the church. I have been active in our denomination for many years. I love our church and I love our denomination. I have never regretted the years I have spent serving the Lord."

I smiled as he was speaking. I took note that there was not one word about sin, not one mention of Christ, and not one syllable about faith. There was nothing but pride and boasting about himself. How could a man like this be saved? How could a man like this exist in a Baptist church for years? How could he be selected to serve in the various offices he had mentioned?

My primary purpose was to help him, but in attempting to do so I knew I would probably offend him.

I asked him, "Where does Christ fit in your testimony? Who is He and what has He done in the matter of your salvation?"

He blushed a little, realizing he should have mentioned Christ, but then his further answer given at this point would have been best left unspoken.

"Oh, well, everyone knows that Christ is our example. We are to try to live like him--to be loving and kind as he was. We are to try to help people like he did."

I noticed that he hadn't touched the question concerning Christ's person. So I tried again.

"What is faith? What is it and what is its object?"

His answer concerning faith was no better than his one on Christ.

"Faith is the confidence that God loves us and has given us power within ourselves to live up to his commandments so that we might be Christians."

I tried again.

"What is evangelism?"

"Evangelism is the work of the church to bring people to the place where they will profess faith in Christ and present themselves for baptism and join the church. Sometimes it takes a lot of love and pleading to get people to make a profession of faith, so our preaching should constantly set before them the advantages of being a Christian and living a good life so they will want to profess faith in Christ and follow him."

I spent about an hour thereafter trying to explain the Biblical plan of salvation, but there was no possibility of penetrating his thought and system. I spoke of sin, faith, Christ, heaven, hell, and many other Biblical subjects. I sought to teach him, plead with him, challenge him, and even shock him, but he could not understand the points I was trying to make. He was convinced he was saved and acceptable to God, and was closed in his mind even to the plainest of Scripture.

Though he didn't seem to understood the particulars of what I was saying, he did get one thing clear--that I was convinced that his view of the plan of salvation was not Biblical.

He said rather shocked, "Are you trying to tell me that you don't think I am saved?"

I wasn't going to get into another Miss Lilly accusation, but then I wasn't going to let him escape the dilemma.

"I am not going to tell you whether you are saved or not. I am telling you what Scripture says, and you must compare what you have stated you believe to be the way of salvation with the Scripture, and if it is contradicted by Scripture, then you are not saved. The Scriptures must be your judge now as they will be in eternity."

It was obvious that he was somewhat shaken. I had taken him from his offensive challenge against me and put him in a defensive posture.

Finally he prepared to leave, promising me that they would give me a month to consider these petitions and resign before bringing them before the church for a formal vote. He acted as if he was being generous and kind by giving such a long period of time to resign.

I assured him I would have to follow the Lord's leadership in the matter. I warned him he was putting himself in a dangerous position by circulating such a petition challenging God's servant. I also told him he had better have his ducks in a row if he ever brought those petitions before the church or he might be in for a surprise or two himself.

This last statement shook him. He couldn't imagine what I had in mind.

The rest of the day I found myself marvelling and asking the question how one could be a member of a Baptist church and never have been saved. I understood there could never be a perfect church on this earth--that it, perfect in the sense that everyone was truly saved, not that everyone lived a perfect life. Even among the twelve there was a Judas.

But surely we could do better than we had done in the past. Had we been too eager to accept people into the church? Had we told people they were saved, when they actually were not? Had we corrupted the church by our false evangelistic practices? Had we allowed the matter to deteriorate to the place where we had little or no membership requirements either to become a member of the church or to remain as a member of the church?

I knew I didn't have all the answers, but I also realized I had found the subject for our next deacons' meeting.

And yes, Garth Duncan definitely became a point of prayer-concern in the days that followed!

I WAS A WANDERING SHEEP

I was a wandering sheep,
    I did not love the fold,
I did not love the Shepherd's voice,
    I would not be controlled;
I was a wayward child,
    I did not love my home,
I did not love the Father's voice,
    I loved afar to roam.

The Shepherd sought His sheep,
    The Father sought His child,
They followed me o'er vale and hill,
    O'er deserts waste and wild;
They found me nigh to death,
    Famished, and faint, and lone;
They bound me with the bands of love,
    They saved the wandering one.

I was a wandering sheep,
    I would not be controlled;
But now I love the Shepherd's voice,
    I love, I love the fold!
I was a wayward child;
    I once preferred to roam;
But now I love my Father's voice,
    I love, I love His home.

---Horatius Bonar

CHAPTER 13

WHAT DOCTRINE OF SALVATION ARE WE PREACHING?

But though we, or an angel from heaven,
preach any other gospel unto you
than that which we have preached unto you,
let him be accursed.
Galatians 1:8

The following Sunday was uneventful (compared with what had been happening), except that several more of the opposing party began to show themselves, at least in the Sunday morning services.

Garth Duncan was there and even took a few signatures for his petition before and after the services. He did it openly almost taunting me with his action. His action only made me pray for him all the more.

All the next week my thinking pointed to the Thursday night deacons' meeting. I wondered if we might not and should not be meeting more than once a week. But time was a factor in the matter, not only for the deacons, but also for me. I had freed up my schedule to some extent as I had dropped out of school until this matter was over.

On Thursday evening we gathered once again, and as on the previous meeting night, all six of the deacons were present. We began with a season of prayer asking God to guide us through the evening and through the entire situation facing us. All the men prayed, which caused my heart to rejoice even further.

Finally, I rose to address them.

"Men, last week we saw that it is possible for one to be religious and yet be lost, Yes, it is possible for one to be even a church member and be lost, that is, not know Jesus Christ. And such a person, though lost, may be deceived themselves, and think they are actually saved."

I summarized further Matthew 7:21-23 as we had set forth its truth from the previous week.

Then I raised the question for the evening.

"My next concern, a concern which the Lord has driven home even deeper this week, is how one can become a member of a Baptist church and yet have never been saved."

I reminded them we were speaking of Baptists now because Baptists had been known in their history as strong proponents of the strong necessity of regenerate church membership.

"Please understand," I continued, "that the task of receiving church members will never be honed to perfection. That is, we can never come to the place where everyone who unites with the church is truly saved. Some lost person or persons will always slip through the doors however hard we may try to keep the doors Scripturally pure. But what we are concerned with this evening is, how is it that a church or churches (to remind us that we are not just speaking of First Baptist Church of Collegetown but of others like us) can come to the place where they have hundreds of inactive and non-resident members while only a few of its membership are evidencing faithful attendance at its public services?"

I knew I didn't have to give them statistics--they were aware of the problem, but still I gave them so they could speak with exactness in any discussions they would have with others.

"Just now we have a total of 1223 names on our membership roll. Of this number we have addresses on 893. We could probably come up with addresses on more than that with some effort, and we are planning to seek to locate them all, but that is the number just now before any special push is attempted."

I continued.

"Now, out of that 893 we can find, about 63 are somewhat faithful in attendance, that is, they attend at least one service a week. The remainder, which totals 830, come only occasionally or never at all."

I had their complete attention as I moved into the real challenge I was seeking to make.

"Now the real question is two-fold. First, how many of these 830 are really saved? And, second, how did these who are members who are lost even get to be members of the church? Just this week I sat with a man who is a member of our church, and found out that he has no understanding of the truth of the gospel or of the message of salvation, yet he is convinced he is saved."

Without identifying him, I shared with them our conversation pointing out how unscriptural he was in his understanding of the gospel, and his absolute confidence in his possession of salvation.

My question was to be expected.

"How did he get to be a member of this church? How has he remained a member so long with such an unscriptural understanding of the gospel?"

My audience was silent, perhaps because anything they might say would incriminate themselves for allowing whatever it was that had contributed to his condition.

In the time that remained I set before them the reasons or conditions which would allow a church to come to the place where they were accepting and continuing to allow lost people on a wholesale basis into their membership.

1. Doctrinal failure will open the doors of the church to lost people.

When a church or people lose the proper understanding of the content of the gospel, they are opening the doors of the church for the acceptance of the lost.

When a church or people lose their understanding of the **sinfulness of man**, the work of evangelism is destroyed. Why? Because if no mention is made of sin or an incorrect understanding of sin is harbored, how can people be forgiven of their sin, saved from their sin, and delivered from the power and guilt of sin, which is what the gospel is all about? Thus the church will receive not saved sinners but lost sinners. But the problem is compounded even to a greater degree because these lost sinners who have no clear understanding of the doctrine of man's sin in the plan of salvation will think they are Christians, and will have an improper view of what it is to be a Christian, and will go about to make others Christians in the false manner in which they think they were made Christians. But how can we speak of salvation if there is no concept of salvation from sin?

When a church or people lose their understanding of the **person and work of Christ**, the work of evangelism is destroyed also. Why? Because Christ is the Savior of sinners. To be able to save sinners He must be seen as the God-man who lived a perfect life to satisfy the demands of the law of God, and died a substitutionary death bearing our sins. To see Him as a good man or even a perfect man who is only our example denies the basic heart of the gospel--that He is the Savior of sinners.

When a church or people lose their understanding of the **definition and place of faith** in salvation, the work of evangelism is short-circuited also. Faith is only true faith as exercised in the context of a true understanding of sin. Faith must have as its object a true concept of the person and work of Christ. Faith must be seen as more than intellectual assent or mental agreement with a few facts about the gospel. Faith must be accompanied by repentance, that is, a turning from sin. True faith will result in a changed life and the granting of a new heart with new desires and new capabilities of understanding spiritual matters.

When one or all of these key doctrines in the plan of salvation is lost, the understanding of salvation in the mind of a man drifts in the direction of ignoring sin, exalting Christ as more of an example to us than as our Savior (Deliverer) from sin, and the robbing of faith of its true object and end, causing us to center faith upon ourselves with some foggy or even non-existent end leaving us with a sort of "faith in faith" idea.

Anyone accepted into a church on the basis of such an understanding of doctrine will enter the church lost and not saved. As they reproduce themselves the corruption of the church will continue.

2. <u>Practical failure will open the doors of the church to the lost</u>.

Usually church practice flows from the doctrine a church holds. I suppose it would not be impossible for a church to hold a proper view of salvation, yet have inconsistent membership practices.

On the other hand, when a church leaves the correct understanding of the above doctrinal areas, it is impossible to have proper membership requirements and practices.

For example, if one no longer holds to a proper view of salvation, the reality of regenerate membership is lost, and the church will begin to accept lost people.

Once having lost the concept of regenerate membership for entrance into the church, it cannot be expected that a church will hold its membership responsible to give evidence of regeneration in the everyday working of the life of the church. In simple words, if they were accepted as members on the basis of weak and false doctrine, they will be dealt with as members on the same basis. Such will result in little if any accountability in their daily lives and in their responsibility to the church.

I could have said more, but the time had come for our discussion. I asked someone to summarize what I had said.

Ed Schuster spoke up.

"A true doctrine of salvation leads to the correct requirements for church membership which lead to proper accountability of the members of the body in its daily life."

Conrad Spratt put it in the negative.

"A false doctrine of salvation leads to the wrong requirements for church membership which leads to little if any accountability of the members of the body in the daily outworking of the life of the church."

I left them with a final question which we did not answer.

"What do these principles say about the doctrine of salvation which has been preached in the past by the First Baptist Church of Collegetown?"

CHAPTER 14

WILL THE IMPURE CLEANSE THEMSELVES?

*Can the Ethiopian change his skin,
or the leopard his spots?
Then may you also do good,
that are accustomed to do evil.*
Jeremiah 13:23

So far in the meeting with the deacons we had concluded that our church was impure in its membership, perhaps even filled with lost people, because the church in times past had left the true doctrine of salvation. The question we faced now was how a church, once it has lost its purity, once it has become exceedingly impure, could ever regain its purity.

In case anyone thought such cleansing would be easy, it had to be remembered that any action leading to purification of the church would have to be approved by the church. This meant that the impure would have to agree that they were impure and needed cleansing, and that they would have to approve all actions to bring the purification. One could hardly expect that to take place.

So, where do we go from here? What plan of action could we possibly recommend which the impure membership would approve to bring discipline upon itself?

The unwillingness of the impure of the membership of the church to cleanse themselves was shown again over the next weekend. About thirty of the adults of their group stalked into the church and refused to go to the designated Sunday School classes. They allowed their children to go to the correct classes, but they set themselves up as a Sunday School class without any authority from the church and with a self-appointed teacher.

They warned us that if we tried to put them out, there would be trouble, or that if we sought to bring the matter before the church they would rally and out-vote us. They added that they were going to take over the church anyway very soon, so we had just as well get used to it. They stated that they had the votes to defeat us, and even if we were to win the vote they were right and were going to do as they pleased.

Great Baptists, these people! Acting without church approval. Stating that they didn't care about church approval or action. Yet at the same time, they went about speaking in glowing terms of their denominational loyalty and declaring what great Baptists they were. They heralded to all who would listen, including denominational leaders, that I was not true to the denomination.

Understandably, when we met the next Thursday evening the question of what we could do was a real and pressing one. The boldness of the opposition was building, as were their numbers, and we were approaching quickly the promised time they would present their petition and ask for my removal.

As we gathered the deacons were buzzing over something. When I asked what, they all held up a piece of paper with something written on it in large letters.

JUDGE NOT LEST YOU BE JUDGED!
Matthew 7:1

I asked them to turn to Matthew 18:15. I also asked one of them to read that verse to me.

Sam Booker read,

Moreover, if thy brother shall trespass against thee, go and tell him his fault between thee and him alone; if he shall hear thee, thou hast gained they brother.

Silence followed till I spoke.

"How can one do what Matthew 18:15 says without drawing some kind of conclusions about matters and without making some kind of judgements about the actions of your brother?"

Silence followed again till I continued.

"Let me state it another way. If we are forbidden to make ANY kind of judgment regarding our brother's actions, as some have interpreted Matthew 7:1, how can one conclude when or if a brother has transgressed against him? And how could we go to him and tell him he has sinned, if we cannot make any kind of conclusion or judgment that he has sinned?"

They continued to listen intently.

"Obviously, this verse does not mean we are to make no spiritual judgments at all--ever world without end. The Bible is full of too many admonitions for believers and Christ's church to know the truth, to preach the truth, to defend the truth, to recognize false teachers, to expel false teachers and on and on. In fact another verse tells us to 'Judge not according to appearance, but judge righteous judgment'."

"Then what does Matthew 7:1 mean?" Eli Melton asked.

"It means we are not to judge others in a super-critical, self-righteous, hypocritical, censorious manner. We must make proper spiritual judgments, but do not do so, even if the conclusions are accurate, in a self-righteous, hypocritical manner. Do what God demands us to do as individuals and as a church in standing for and defending the truth, in the expulsion of falsehood and in the discipline of the church membership, but do it in a spirit of love and not with a harsh, bitter, critical, unforgiving, self-righteous spirit as if we were God or as if we could never fail or fall."

Conrad Spratt continued to show his depth of spiritual understanding as he spoke next, addressing all the men.

"Men, many of the membership are using Matthew 7:1 to urge us to make no spiritual conclusions about anyone or anyone's beliefs. Yet is it not strange and inconsistent that they are judging our pastor in his preaching, in his relation and loyalty to the denomination, in his view of salvation, and in his convictions concerning what the church should be doing and where it should be headed?"

I couldn't have agreed with him more thoroughly and I couldn't have said it better. All the men not only nodded in agreement, but they also broke forth in rejoicing as they understood the proper understanding of this passage.

I summarized our discussion as follows:

1. If Matthew 7:1 means that we cannot make any kind of judgment or draw any kind of conclusion concerning anything, how can the opposition be judging the pastor and be walking in obedience to the verse they love to quote?

2. If Matthew 7:1 means we cannot make any kind of judgment or draw any kind of conclusion, then are they not sinning in their drawing of conclusions and judgments against the pastor and even us as we follow his leadership and they criticize us all?

3. Obviously the verse cannot mean to judge no one about anything or to draw no conclusions about anything or it would completely paralyze the church in its legitimate work of performing its God-given task to guard the church from falsehood and impurity.

4. The only consistent meaning of the verse is that it disallows false and improper judgment, hypercritical or censorious judgment, or harsh and bitter improper judgment.

Bob Motley blurted out when I was finished, "Boy, am I glad to learn this. I'll sure be prepared when somebody hits me with Matthew 7:1 again!"

I didn't have the heart to tell him, but he would find out very soon, that these folks really don't care what the Bible says. They will use it when it fits their purposes, even if they have to twist it. But when the Bible directly contradicts their beliefs or actions, they are very skilled at ignoring it.

We agreed that the day of decision was fast approaching. We decided to meet Saturday evening also.

We didn't know what to do to bring purity, but it was obvious that the impure would not cleanse themselves.

CHAPTER 15

DO YOU WANT TO TEAR
THAT CHURCH TO PIECES?

*Hath the Lord as great delight
in burnt offering and sacrifices,
as in obeying the voice of the Lord?
Behold to obey is better than sacrifice,
and to hearken than the fat of rams.*
I Samuel 15:22

On the Friday before our Saturday meeting more pressure from the opposition was placed upon us. I was paid a visit by an official from our state Baptist convention. It seems that the opposition had gone to see him about the "troubles" at First Baptist Church.

I had met him previously but I am sure he would not have known who I was except for the visit by the opposition party. He called on me in my office, and after the usual introductory moment of conversation, he got to the point.

"Brother Pointer, be assured that I am here at the best interest of the church. Understand also that I only wish to help both sides of the controversy in your church. One group has come to ask my help, and I always stand open and ready to help any group of Baptists requesting such."

I nodded, but it was a neutral nod for I wished to express neither agreement or disagreement, especially since neither I nor the leadership of the church had invited his intervention.

"Young man, let me begin by expressing to you my joy at the honor this church has bestowed upon you in calling you as pastor. This is as fine a church as our denomination has in the state. I'm sure you want to do a good job here as pastor, because it will set the stage for all your future ministry in our denomination."

Though I may have been young, I saw right through him. He was buttering me up, on the one hand, and he was putting me down on the other by referring to my youth. And he was putting pressure on me to follow whatever suggestions he might give me by mentioning my future in the denomination. I was concerned that so many of the men of our denomination were so career-minded. Nothing was as important as one's career--not even the truth.

He continued.

"Young man, take it from one who has spent many more years in the ministry and in our denomination than you have. A preacher needs to get his feet planted on firm ground, know what way he is going, and press on."

I said nothing, but thought to myself that he was a master of cliches and generalities. Yet, obviously, he was preparing me for the particulars.

He finally looked like he might get to the point.

"It has come to my attention that you have some real problems in this church. Now, please understand that I have no desire to interfere in the affairs of a local church, nor do I have any authority over you or the church. Such an idea would be against Baptist polity."

I was getting a little weary of his verbosity and inability to get to the point, so I sought to push him to his point.

"Brother Adams, let's cut the small talk and get to the point. What is it that you and the visitors you had are troubled about in the life of our church?"

"Well," he stuttered (perhaps he was not used to being brought up short), "I think the main concern, though there are several, is that they are afraid you are going to install some new practices in receiving and retaining membership in the church. There's talk of 'cleansing the rolls' and 'purifying the church' which really is troubling some of your people."

I stretched and changed positions in my chair, and let him talk.

"Now I think I know something about Baptist practices. I've been a Baptist all my life. I attended a Baptist college and seminary. I have pastored several Baptist churches for a total of 20 years. I have been on the staff of the state convention for 15 years now. So, you see, I should know something of Baptist life and doctrine and practice."

He smiled and I smiled in return but I said nothing. I thought, "Okay, so you have a Baptist pedigree."

He continued with a condescending air--he was the old pro telling the young rookie how it was.

"You do understand, Brother Pointer, that we as Baptists have no creed but the Bible, but on the other hand, we do have some well established practices of the reception and dismissal of church members. Membership is based solely on a profession of faith, whereby one is then baptized and received into the membership of the church body. Any extensive training and teaching should follow baptism and church membership and not precede it."

I decided to let him finish before challenging him.

"As far as dismissal from a church body, there are several ways a church removes members from its roll. (1) One can transfer to another church of like faith and order by letter; (2) Or a name is removed if the church is informed by a church of another denomination that an individual has united with that church; (3) Or a name is removed at death or when the church learns one has died even if that information comes several years later; (4) And, finally, an individual can ask for his name to be removed and a church usually honors that request. To my knowledge these are the only grounds for removing a name from a Baptist Church."

I wondered what knowledge he had of church history, since he had never heard of removing a name through church discipline. I decided again to let him continue.

"Now, Brother Pointer, my opinion is that what you are attempting to lead this church to do is not Scriptural nor does it fit the long tradition of Baptist procedures and practices relative to church membership. I would advise you to drop any such plan and return to these historic Baptist practices, and seek to renew the harmony and unity in your church. There is no end to the possibility of growth and blessing you can see on this church if you will desist from this unscriptural and nonbaptistic practice you are trying to establish. But if you do persist, there is also no way to estimate the damage you will do to this church and to your own future ministry."

He was finally finished. I thanked him for his concern, and then began my reply by a series of questions.

"Brother Adams, have you ever heard of the <u>Summary of Church Discipline</u> adopted by the Charleston Baptist Association in South Carolina?"

An amazed look came across his face. I added further information for him.

"Though it is older, it is a highly respected and recognized Baptist document which was used by not only the churches of the Charleston Association but it reflects the convictions and practices of other Baptist churches in past history."

He began to twist impatiently in his chair, but I kept talking.

"It speaks of requirements for church membership and the need to be sure people meet those requirements before joining. It speaks of duties of church members and the need to hold people accountable in fulfilling these duties. And it speaks of the discipline of church members for their failure in fulfilling these responsibilities. The discipline includes rebuke or admonition, suspension, and excommunication."

I paused for any comment he might have.

"Oh, that's old stuff--too old for modern Baptists to follow!"

I didn't intend to be mean, but I wasn't going to let him off the hook.

"Brother Adams, are you familiar with Matthew 18:15-18, or II Thessalonians 3:6, or II Corinthians 5:1-7, or Galatians 6:1, or I Timothy 6:3-5? All these verses speak of the church's duty and responsibility to practice discipline and seek to hold its members accountable for the living of a holy and godly life. So please, do not tell me that what we are hoping to do here at First Baptist Church is neither Scriptural nor Baptistic. The Bible and Baptist history are on our side and not on yours. Your argument may work with laymen and pastors who know nothing of Baptist history, and with those who are unfamiliar with Scriptural standards. But for the one who is informed you don't have a leg to stand on."

I spoke with a smile hoping to take some of the tension from the situation, but I'm not sure it had worked. I was a young preacher who wasn't supposed to know very much. He was an old Baptist veteran who surely, he thought, would know more than I did. But he had no response because he had no defense, unless he torpedoed Baptist history and cast doubt upon the Scripture.

I wasn't sure whether he said what he had out of ignorance of Baptist history and Bible doctrine, or if he thought he could misrepresent both to prove his conviction and not be called on it. I concluded that he had spoken out of ignorance, or to be kinder, out of a knowledge of Baptists only from the past fifty years or so with no real knowledge of anything past his historical perspective. He automatically assumed that the Baptist practices of his lifetime were the historic Baptist views and practices of all their history.

Whatever the case he was not happy with me. I had stood up to him and perhaps even embarrassed him.

As he left I assured him that we were only seeking to do what was right as revealed in Scripture, and we were convinced that what was Scriptural was also Baptistic historically. We were not trying to make trouble, but if trouble came as we sought to stand for the Word of God, we would have to face it and trust the Lord to accomplish His purpose.

He shook his head in sorrow and said, "What you are doing will tear this church to pieces!"

THE FEW

The easy roads are crowded
    And the level roads are jammed;
The pleasant little rivers
    With the drifting folks are crammed.

But off yonder where it's rocky
    Where you get a better view,
You will find the ranks are thinning
    And the travelers are few.

But the steeps that call for courage
    And the task that's hard to do,
In the end result in glory
    For the never wavering few.

        ---Author Unknown

CHAPTER 16

WHERE DOES THE BIBLE SPEAK OF CHURCH DISCIPLINE?

*Blessed is the man
who walketh not in the counsel of the ungodly,
nor standeth in the way of sinners,
nor sitteth in the seat of the scornful.
Psalms 1:1*

I really didn't like Saturday night meetings for a church or a pastor. I liked to spend Saturday evening relaxing and getting my mind and body prepared for the long day Sunday, especially after a busy week.

But this Saturday evening was necessary because the day of the oppositions' deadline for me to resign was quickly approaching. It was just two weeks away. That really didn't leave us much time.

I began that Saturday evening's meeting with some clear ground rules. I was going to set before them several passages of Scripture. I would read each one and then comment briefly on each set of verses. I asked them to please save their comments until the end of the total presentation. My purpose, I told them in sharing these verses was to show them that the Bible teaches a church should be a disciplined body.

We began with Matthew 18:15-17.

15 Moreover, if thy brother shall trespass against thee, go and tell him his fault between thee and him alone; if he shall hear thee, thou hast gained thy brother.

16 But if he will not hear thee, then take with thee one or two more, that in the mouth of two or three witnesses every word may be established.

17 And if he shall neglect to hear them, tell it unto the church; but if he neglects to hear the church, let him be unto thee as a heathen man and a publican.

I noted for them the following facts from this passage:

1. Believers in the church should be concerned about sin in the lives of other members of the church.

2. A believer in a church who is sinned against by another member of that church has a responsibility to confront the sinning brother while the two of them are alone, hoping to correct him and restore the broken fellowship between them.

3. If the sinning brother of the church refuses to hear the brother who is seeking to correct him and restore him as he is approached alone, then the concerned brother is to visit him again, only this time he is to take two or three witnesses so that every word may be established.

4. If the sinning brother refuses to hear on the second visit with the presence of two or three witnesses, the matter is to be taken to the church in public meeting.

5. If the sinning brother refuses to hear the church, then he is to be looked upon and treated as a lost man.

I did ask for a response here in the form of a yes or no answer.

"According to Jesus, do church members have a responsibility to hold other members of the church accountable for the way they live?"

They answered with a strong, "Yes."

"According to Jesus, does the church itself have a responsibility to hold its members accountable for the way they live?"

Again they responded with a strong, "Yes."

"According to Jesus, does the church have a responsibility to discipline one who refuses to hear the church as it seeks to carry out its work of correction?"

Again the answer was "Yes!"

Our next passage was I Corinthians 5:1-7. I could see on their faces some questions, or at least a desire to express themselves, but I reminded them of our ground rules and moved to the second set of verses.

> *1   It is reported commonly that there is fornication among you, and such fornication as is not so much as named among the Gentiles, that one should have his father's wife.*
>
> *2   And ye are puffed up, and have not rather mourned, that he that hath done this deed might be taken away from among you.*
>
> *3   For I verily, as absent in the body but present in the spirit have judged already as though I were already present, concerning him that hath done this deed.*
>
> *4   In the name of our Lord Jesus Christ , when you are gathered together, and my spirit, with the power of our Lord Jesus Christ,*
>
> *5   To deliver such an one unto Satan for the destruction of the flesh, that the spirit may be saved in the day of the Lord Jesus.*
>
> *6   Your glorying is not good. Know ye not that a little leaven leaveneth the whole lump?*
>
> *7   Purge out, therefore, the old leaven, that ye may be a new lump, as ye are unleavened. For even Christ, our passover, is sacrificed for us.*

Again I summarized the key ideas of the passage as follows:

1. Paul notes that the Corinthian Church has a problem in that one of its members is living with a very severe sin in his life.

2. Paul scolds them for having done nothing about it.

3. Paul instructs them as to what they must do (even should have done) to discipline the sinner and thus purge the church of the stain brought by this member.

4. Paul warns that failure to purge the body (the church) will result in further sin in the body as a little leaven will leaven the whole lump. That is to say, that failure to hold one man accountable for his sin, will bring a relaxing of standards of holiness and righteousness to the whole church, until the entire church is living loose and ungodly lives.

Quiz time followed as I asked several questions.

"According to Paul, should a church be concerned about the kind of life its members live, especially if one falls into deep sin?"

"Yes," they responded, getting louder with each response.

"According to Paul, should a church discipline a member who has fallen into a deep sin?"

"Yes!" they rang out again.

According to Paul, are there consequences to the church if it fails to do what it should in disciplining a member?"

"Yes!" they chimed again.

"What?" I asked, changing pace a little.

"Eventually the whole church will become lax in living the Christian life and others, it seems, will follow this sinning member into his and even other sins of severe nature," stated Bill Ashton.

Our next verse was Galatians 6:1. Our time was moving quickly, so I hurried on.

"Men, listen to Galatians 6:1."

> *Brethren, if a man be overtaken in a fault, ye who are spiritual restore such a one in a spirit of meekness, considering thyself, lest thou also be tempted.*

I called to their attention again that here is a clear command to deal with sin in the body. The spiritual ones of the congregation (obviously the leadership) must have a concern and love and meekness to restore a brother who has fallen into sin. Sin cannot be ignored in the body.

Our next passage was I Timothy 6:3-5. By now they were about to come apart at the seams with a desire to comment on these verses. But I moved on and read the verses.

> *3   If any man teach otherwise, and consent not to wholesome words, even the words of our Lord Jesus Christ, and to the doctrine which is according to godliness,*
> *4   He is proud, knowing nothing, but doting about questions and strifes of words, of which cometh envy, strife, railings, evil surmisings,*
> *5   Perverse disputings of men of corrupt minds, and destitute of the truth, supposing that gain is godliness; from such withdraw thyself.*

I had to give a brief explanation of this passage.

"Men, this passage speaks of both doctrine and life-style. It is true that these words are addressed to Timothy. And it is true that when Paul says to withdraw from such a person on these doctrinal and practical grounds, he addresses not a church but a single individual for he speaks in the second person singular. But it would be rather unbelievable that a leader of a church, such as Timothy, should withdraw fellowship from such a person, and yet the church should not."

My final verse was II Thessalonians 3:6, and I read it as follows:

> *Now we command you, brethren, in the name of our Lord Jesus Christ, that you withdraw yourselves from every brother that walketh disorderly and not after the tradition which he received of us.*

I noted several points from this verse.

1. Paul sets forth this command in the name of the Lord
    Jesus Christ, that is, by the authority of Christ.

2. Paul is addressing a church, the church at
    Thessalonica, and the command is in the plural.
    That is, you (plural) withdraw yourselves (plural),
    etc.

3. Paul commands them to withdraw from every
    brother who does not walk according to the proper
    order or requirements.

There was so much more which could have been said
and needed to be said about these verses. But they were
about to burst, because I had held them back from speaking
for so long.

We spent the remainder of our time discussing these
verses. I was overjoyed to see their acceptance of these
truths. I was afraid that one of them might be like the
denominational worker who visited me--fearful of the results
of seeking to apply Scripture to the life of a church when
such had not been done for so long.

We also decided, after a time of prayer, that we must
start somewhere in our church to try to apply these verses.
We agreed the place to start was with Miss Lilly. She was
the catalyst who had spurred the problem, and her accusation
was continuing to stir it. We had to face her and call her to
account.

We prayed that we might act in love and meekness as the
Scripture commanded. We prayed Miss Lilly might be open
to hear us.

CHAPTER 17

WHAT WILL THE CHURCH DO WITH MISS LILLY?

Rivers of waters run down mine eyes,
because they keep not thy law.
Psalms 119:136

I was not looking forward to visiting Miss Lilly on the next Monday evening, but I knew it had to be done. One comfort was that I wasn't going in blind as to the possibilities, and I wasn't going alone. Conrad Spratt, the chairman of the deacons, was with me as we approached her home.

I had found out some facts about her since my visit with her in the hospital. She was a widow woman. Her husband had been dead about ten years. They had no children. He had been a lawyer and seemed to have done well financially.

I wondered, as we knocked on the door, if she would answer, especially if she turned on a porch light and looked out the window to see who was calling. It was dark, being winter and about 7:15 in the evening. Some lights were on, so she appeared to be home. Finally, we saw a curtain open slightly, and knew she was peering out.

Conrad Spratt spoke up, since her respect for me wasn't much.

"Miss Lilly, it's Conrad Spratt and the pastor. Could we visit with you for a few moments?"

We heard the locks on the door being unfastened, so it appeared we might get a hearing after all. When the door opened, she invited us in, but she said almost nothing.

When we were seated in the living room, she took on her fake sorrowful personality which she had used to dupe her friends in the hospital.

Before we could say anything, she spoke up sadly.

"I hope you men have come to apologize for what the pastor said to me in the hospital. I have been so upset since then that I can hardly sleep."

Conrad then spoke to confront her with her sin.

"Miss Lilly, we have no desire for you to be hurt. But I think you had better know that we have proof that our pastor never said what you have accused him of saying. You not only have a drinking problem that you need to face, but you also have a problem with telling the truth."

She exploded again and the personality changed also.

"So, I'm not only a drinker, but now you're accusing me of being a liar. Wait till the people of the church hear about this--they'll vote for him to go for sure."

He tried again.

"Miss Lilly, do you mean to tell us that it doesn't bother you if a young pastor is being constantly attacked, that he may have to leave this church, or that the church could be torn apart, solely on the basis of a lie you have told about him? Do you have no conscience? Do you have no concern for others--if not for him, then for the church?"

She answered, but she didn't really face the issue.

"Well, I guess if I'm no longer welcome in my own church, I'll just have to go and join another Baptist church in this town. Just bring me my letter and I'll be glad to be out of First Baptist Church."

I let Conrad continue to handle the matter.

"We can't do that, Miss Lilly. We give letters only to churches. And at this point we could not give you a letter of recommendation until you have made the matter right with the church. You are in rebellion against the church in that you are in rebellion against the leadership of the church. Any church you would try to join would get a letter from us, but it would not be a letter of recommendation, but a letter of information concerning what you have done. We could not and would not send a letter of recommendation until there has been repentance and restoration."

Conrad was getting ready to show her some of the verses we had discussed Saturday evening, but he never got a chance. She ordered us out of her house and instructed us never to come back.

Conrad informed her that we would have to take this matter before the church Wednesday evening. If she wanted to defend herself and state her case, she needed to be there. We would be ready to accept her repentance or argument, and we would also be ready to present our evidence that she was not telling the truth. The matter of her drinking problem, Conrad informed her, needed no evidence-- everyone knew about it.

Now she was boiling! She ordered us to leave again, but she didn't even see us to the door. She disappeared into another part of the house. As she went she cursed and swore at us using some words I hadn't heard in quite awhile since my conversion. We had tried to pray with her, but she refused, so we left.

We knew the version of the visit which she would tell would probably be a far cry from what actually took place. But at least now I had a witness to substantiate the events and conversation. And Wednesday evening we would bring it before the church.

It seemed like an eternity between Monday evening and Wednesday evening, and yes, the stories flew all over the city. Now it was that the pastor and the deacon had come and told Miss Lilly she was going to die and go to hell if she didn't repent. We knew telephones rung off the hook those two days, because even some of the faithful fifty were called and badgered in behalf of the opposition.

Further harassment was given Terry and me. Phone calls with no one on the other end of the line when we answered were numerous. Several hate letters came in the mail. Several confrontations with people erupted as I simply went about town to perform my duties or complete other personal chores. The ambulance was called again and sent to our house.

As that Wednesday evening hour approached, butterflies began to flutter in my stomach. To be honest, the strain of all of this was beginning to get to me.

Our normal service on Wednesday evening began at 7:00 and consisted of Bible study and prayer. It was usually over about 8:15, and any business hour was after that. As we gathered I noted that the crowd was larger than usual because of the opposition, but not as large as it could have been. Concerned that some of the opposition might skip the first part of Bible study and prayer (they had no heart for these matters), and come only for the business part, Conrad and I decided it might be best to deal with the business first after the reading of Scripture and a brief time of prayer.

I had been preaching through the gospel of Matthew and had just a few weeks ago dealt with Matthew 18:15-17 (that's probably where the opposition was getting the idea we were going to "church" everybody). Thus the faithful fifty or so were familiar with it and of what we needed to do. But I read the passage, and then called on Conrad Spratt to lead in prayer and for Bill Ashton to moderate the meeting. Miss Lilly was not present for the meeting.

Then Conrad Spratt presented our case against Miss Lilly. He informed the people that she had several problems we must recognize and deal with.

1. She has a problem with alcohol--again, something we did not have to prove, but something everyone knew.

2. She has a problem with telling the truth in that she had lied about the pastor and his conversation with her in the hospital and she had now lied about the conversation with her in her home the previous Monday evening when two witnesses were present.

3. She has a problem with gossip in that she had heralded her lies and false accusations to many in the church membership and others outside the church membership.

4. She has a problem with creating factions in the church as many had listened to her and were stirring against the church and its leadership and its appointed and established authority.

5. She has a rebellious spirit in that she had been approached for restoration and reconciliation with the church and its leadership, but she refused to listen and to repent, but swore and cursed at those who had come representing the church to help her.

Conrad set before the congregation the Biblical ground for the actions we had taken and were recommending the church take that evening.

He then stated that in light of these violations against Christ and His body, the deacons were recommending that she be removed from the church membership and be treated like a lost person until there was some evidence of a change of heart and genuine repentance.

Then the fur began to fly!

Men may misjudge thy aim,
Think they have cause to blame,
Say, thou art wrong;
Keep on thy quiet way,
Christ is the judge, not they,
Fear not, be strong.

---Selected

No chance has brought this ill to me;
Tis God's own hand, so let it be.
He seeth what I cannot see.
There is a need-be for each pain
And He one day will make it plain
That earthly loss is heavenly gain.

---Selected

CHAPTER 18

WILL YOU TAKE OUR NAMES OFF THE CHURCH ROLL?

Trust in the Lord with all thine heart,
and lean not unto thine own understanding.
In all thy ways acknowledge him,
and he shall direct thy paths.
Proverbs 3:5-6

When Conrad had finished his statement of charges and the recommendation of the deacons, Garth Duncan, the leader of the opposition was the first to speak.

"I would like to move that we delay this recommendation until 8:30 this evening. Some of the church membership were under the impression that the business action of the church would follow the usual Wednesday night Bible study and prayer."

I thought at the time, "If these people have no interest in Bible study and prayer, how are they qualified to vote concerning the spiritual matters of a church?"

The motion was seconded, the vote was taken and recorded as 53 to 41 against it.

He tried again.

"I move the motion be tabled until next Wednesday evening so we can all have time to think and pray about these matters."

It was clear that he was stalling for time so he could rally his forces. But when the vote was taken, he lost again by the same margin.

Someone else spoke up and demanded to know this evidence which would prove Miss Lilly was lying concerning her hospital visit with the pastor.

The moderator called upon me to speak to that question.

The time had come to reveal the evidence which would prove my innocence.

I called for my two witnesses to come forward.

The wife of Troy Medford, the young policeman I had met at the hospital, and another young lady stepped forward. No one had thought it strange that Bonnie Medford was present. She too had been saved and had been attending with her husband and they were being discipled before uniting with the church. Some may have wondered why the other young lady was there in light of the kind of meeting expected.

I set the stage for their testimony.

"These two young ladies are nurses at the hospital. They work on the same floor where Miss Lilly stayed while she was there. They heard the conversation between me and Miss Lilly at the hospital. They were monitoring Miss Lilly that day on the intercom because she had threatened to commit suicide when she was first brought into the hospital."

I asked one of the ladies to step outside for a few moments while I questioned the other. Eli Melton and his wife escorted her outside the sanctuary for a few minutes.

I turned and addressed Bonnie.

"Did you hear all my conversation with Miss Lilly?"

"Yes, the entire exchange," she replied.

"Did I conduct myself in a proper manner in talking with Miss Lilly during the entire conversation?"

Again she nodded yes.

"Did I tell Miss Lilly that if she did not repent of her sin she would die and go to hell?" I asked.

"Never!" she stated emphatically.

"In your own words, tell us what did happen in the hospital room," I suggested.

She told the whole story, mentioning my concern expressed for the patient, her change of personalities from sweet to nasty back to sweet and pitiful before her friends.

When she was finished, the other girl was brought in and she told the exact same story.

I turned the meeting back over to the moderator and after several other futile attempts to stall or to discredit the witnesses, someone called for the vote, and the opposition was defeated again by the same margin.

About the time the vote ended, the remaining members of the opposition entered the church. They were furious that they had missed the vote on Miss Lilly, and of course, they blamed me. At this point I saw something I hope I never have to see again. They began to yell and scream at the moderator and at me. Words of all flavor and expression, including curse words, began to flow from their mouths. I was frightened that one of them might attack one of us.

Then they took an action out of fury which they had not fully thought out. They asked that their names be removed from the church roll also as a sign of support for Miss Lilly. And with that even before a vote could be taken, they walked out vowing they would never set foot in that church again!

The faithful quickly obliged them with a vote that rendered their request. We compiled a list of those present before dismissing just to be sure we didn't miss anyone.

We tarried a little while in prayer, rejoicing, yet knowing that Satan doesn't quit easily.

It was with that thought and knowledge that Terry and I left the church. I knew the battle wasn't over! I just didn't know what they would do next. Would it be revenge? Or would they change their minds and try to be reinstated into the church? Would they take it out on me? or on Terry? or on the church building? or on the parsonage?

I walked through the dark to the car with much apprehension remembering not only the first beating, but also noting that the two (I was certain of one and fairly sure of the other) who had beaten me were, along with their mothers, among those we had dismissed from the membership that evening.

We got to the car alright, but I was still apprehensive as we drove through the streets to get home. Who knew or who could guess what they would do next?

When I pulled within sight of the parsonage, I noticed a truck parked in front of the parsonage. I didn't know what to do. I didn't want to pull into the driveway and get out before knowing who it was. I had no way of knowing how many more were around the corner waiting to descend on the house once I had gotten out. Who knew what weapons they might have?

I told Terry to get down in the front seat, and I drove past the truck. One passenger, that I could see, was sitting on the driver's side of the truck. I turned around and pulled up to the truck headed in the opposite direction and with my driver's side to his driver's side. I kept the car in gear and my foot on the gas pedal, intending to floor it and get out of there at the first sight of trouble.

I rolled the window down slightly and demanded, "Who is it?"

"Preacher," the reply came, "its Barton Medford. I need to see you."

It was one of my attackers! Still not trusting him, I instructed him.

"Meet me at Handy's Hamburgers."

With that I sped away knowing that if he was there on mischief he would not come because the place is well lit and well populated. On the other hand, if he was serious, we could talk even in the parking lot if he was not wanting to be seen with me.

To my amazement he drove into the parking lot just a few seconds after I had arrived. He was by himself. After getting out of his car, he approached mine and wanted to know if he could get in the back seat and talk.

I wasn't certain yet that I could trust him. I asked Terry to go in and get us a coke. I figured I could find out in a few minutes if he intended any harm, and if so it would only be against me and not Terry. If I saw anything suspicious I could hopefully warn Terry of the danger before she got back in the car.

Again, surprisingly I found a very troubled young man in the back seat of my car. It was obvious as we talked that the Lord was working in another heart.

CHAPTER 19

WHY DON'T CHURCHES GUARD THEIR PURITY FROM THE BEGINNING?

*If anyone will come after me, let him deny himself,
and take up his cross daily, and follow me.*
Luke 9:23

The conversation with Barton Medford in the backseat of my car began with an apology. He was deeply sorry that he had been involved in the attack against me. He said he realized it would have been wrong of them to attack me even if I had been guilty, but now that he had found out he had acted on the basis of a lie, he was even more ashamed.

He thanked me for not prosecuting him, because he realized now he could have gone to jail for his action, all of it on the basis of being misled by someone's falsehood to him.

I had several questions for him at this point.

"If this is all true, why did you walk out with the opposition tonight at church?"

"Oh, preacher," he remonstrated, "I may have sat with the opposition, and I may have voted with them on the first couple of ballots, but when I heard the truth about Miss Lilly's accusations against you, I not only quit voting with them, but I did not walk out with them! I stayed. I do want to be a member of the church and do what is right now."

I realized then that somehow in the confusion of that group of people screaming and yelling in their anger we may have missed Barton's decision to remain when they walked out.

For the next hour or so we talked of spiritual matters. I appreciated his taking a stand against the opposition and wanting to remain a member of the church, but I wasn't even sure at this point that he was a Christian. In the process of the conversation, as I showed him verse after verse from the Scriptures, he came to the understanding that he had never been saved. And shortly thereafter, in the back seat of my car, he came to know the Lord.

Then we sat for about another hour talking of what he could expect from his family. He shared with me what a testimony his cousin, Troy (the young policeman), had been to him since he had been saved. He guaranteed me that he understood the difficulty which would follow in seeking to follow Christ against his immediate family, especially at First Baptist Church.

We prayed together (he prayed also) before we parted, and we set up a regular time when we could meet for fellowship and discipleship.

When we got back to the house, it was late and everything was peaceful and quiet, but I realized I had not heard the last of the Miss Lilly problem nor the Medford family.

The next day, a Thursday, was quite uneventful, kind of like the calm after the storm. Perhaps the opposition was weighing the implications of their action the previous evening before making further plans. I wished they would just go and leave us alone.

But Thursday evening was eventful, in that it was the meeting with the deacons. There was subdued rejoicing at what God had done--He had even put it in the hearts of the opposition to remove themselves from the membership of the church so that we would not have to do it.

Yet we cautioned ourselves not to think the battle was over but to walk alertly, and to continue to carry out what God was doing in our midst. We reminded ourselves that there were still hundreds of inactive members on our church roll.

I sensed a need to do three things that evening. First, I wanted to summarize for them what we had seen in our study. Next, I wanted to give them a review of what we were going to study in the future. Last, I wanted to set before them the next move we needed to make from a practical standpoint in continuing the cleansing of the membership roll.

I summarized our past study as follows:

We have seen

1. that one can be very religious and yet be lost.

2. that one can be even a church member and be lost.

3. how one gets to be a lost church member
   --through doctrinal error and unscriptural
   practices slipping into the church polity.

4. that individual Christians have an obligation
   to hold each other accountable for the
   living of a Christian life.

5. that the Church has an obligation
   to hold its members accountable and responsible
   for living a Christian life, including discipline of
   a negative nature if one refuses to respond to the
   Church's teaching and admonition.

Next, I informed them concerning our future study together. I would be setting before them the subject of discipline from two aspects--formative and reformative discipline. Formative discipline is the work the church does when it trains and teaches its new converts and membership prospects. Reformative discipline is the discipline applied after one has been accepted into the membership of the church and yet begins to lag in his life and growth and commitment to Christ and the church.

Finally for that evening, I set before them a plan to follow in seeking to continue the cleansing of the church roll. I suggested that we spend a few weeks trying to complete an accurate listing and address for all our members. The church secretary, along with some volunteer help, could work on that. We already had done a good bit of this job and just needed to finish it concentrating on some whose addresses had been almost impossible to find.

The next move after the compilation of the final list would be to send all the inactive members a letter telling them of our concern for them and our desire that they become involved in the life of the church on a regular basis once again. The letter would invite them to contact us if there were any questions we could answer. Finally, the letter would inform them that if they had not shown any further interest in the Church and its life by a certain date, their names would be removed from the roll.

I drove home that evening exhausted and thinking, "It sure is a lot easier to keep a church pure in the beginning than to try to purify one after years of indifference and corruption."

Then I realized that in one way it may not be easy to keep a church pure from the beginning. Compromise is easier than standing for the truth. It's easier to compromise the doctrine rather than offend someone. It's easier to compromise the commitment required after one makes a profession of faith and joins the church than confront someone. It's easier to compromise the membership standards and requirements and allow more people into the church rather than to hold the standards high and have fewer "joiners" and look bad in the eyes of the denomination, especially when so many are doing so well in numbers, it seems, and when the denominational leaders are pushing for numbers.

It's easier to work in one church as a pastor and play the game of numbers, and then move to a bigger church as a result, and then on up the ladder of ministerial success than to labor faithfully in one church. Moving on keeps one from having to face his evangelistic failures and unregenerate membership. He can simply go to another church and produce the same thing. Let the next guy who follows pay the price of the impurity of the church. Meanwhile, at the new church one can blast the last pastor for his lack of care for the purity of the church while one continues to do the same thing.

I sighed as I drove into my driveway. Surely it's got to stop somewhere. Surely our denomination will wake up someday and realize what it has done and what it is continuing to do. Maybe someday, I thought, I'll write a book on the subject.

CHAPTER 20

WHY DON'T CHURCHES PRACTICE CHURCH DISCIPLINE?

But I keep under my body, and bring it into subjection,
lest that by any means, when I have preached to others,
I myself should be a castaway.
I Corinthians 9:27

I must confess I was not surprised when my secretary buzzed me on Friday morning and said that Garth Duncan, the leader of the opposition group, was in her office and wanted to see me. I knew he was there to tell me of their next move, and I was curious to know what it would be.

When he entered he was quite friendly. I wondered how a man that friendly could be working to stab me in the back, but then perhaps the Lord was giving me a lesson in the deceptiveness of Satan.

After exchanging a few stiff unpleasant pleasantries, he came to the point.

"Pastor, I want to discuss with you what happened the other evening."

I said nothing but let him continue.

"We would like to withdraw our request at the end of the service the other evening--the request to drop our names from the church roll. You surely realize that we acted without thinking. We all have long histories and heritages here. We all grew up here. And our families made their professions and were baptized here. This is the only church many of us have ever known. Our families are buried in the church cemetery and we would like to be buried with them."

The church had originally had a cemetery right beside it when the town was small, but then in later years the cemetery was moved to the outskirts of town. Still the church owned and governed the property and anyone who was a member of the church received a free burial plot. I hadn't even thought the cemetery could become an issue in this battle.

He continued his plea.

"We are even willing to postpone our vote on you as our pastor for a month if the church will reinstate us as members."

I thought to myself, what a twisted view of fairness this guy has. He wants a favor from us, but then he and his group still will proceed with plans to cut my head off--they will only postpone it for a month.

I informed him of the following.

"First, the church has voted and I would not ask them to rescind that vote. As far as I am concerned, it stands. It has saved us the trouble of doing something we probably would have had to do anyway. It also removes a very strong negative faction from the church."

He started to interrupt me, but I asked him to listen till I was finished, as I had listened quietly to him.

"Second, if I were you, I would be ashamed to come here and even make such a request. You have stirred trouble against the leadership and faithful members of this church all the way from the inactive and unspiritual members to the local associational leaders and even to state Baptist officials. You have started a Sunday School class without church authorization, and refuse to shut it down as it continues to meet in brazen rebellion to the desires of this church."

Again, he tried to interrupt me, and I could see the "Mr. Nice Guy" facade was disappearing. I raised my hand indicating I didn't want to hear anything from him and continued.

"I think it would be better for you and your group and any others like you to abide by the action of the church and leave the church. You are not happy here. You are causing trouble for the ones who want to serve the Lord here faithfully, and I see no possibility that the vote of the church can be altered."

I was finished and it didn't take him long to grab the floor and verbally assault me.

"We will not leave this church! I don't care how many times you may vote us out. We are staying and you will eventually leave, believe me! Even if we have to set up an underground church, a church within a church, we will not leave. We will not separate ourselves from our past. We will not separate ourselves against our family. We paid for these buildings! We have worshipped here for years! Hear me, preacher? We will not leave--ever."

With that he walked out in a rage. I couldn't begin to imagine what he would do next.

On Saturday evening the deacons met once again. The hour was critical. We had agreed to meet two nights a week regularly until our task was finished.

I addressed them on several general and introductory matters pertaining to church discipline.

I reviewed for them the difference between formative and reformative discipline. I noted that usually when one hears the word "discipline" he thinks of the second, but that formative discipline is just as important as reformative. In fact, if a church practices formative discipline and has careful policies in receiving members, the matter of reformative discipline is made much easier.

"Formative discipline," I said in review, "is the teaching and training that one gets to form his Christian character and doctrine prior to his joining the church and even following the acceptance into the membership of the church. The church should constantly be concerned that its members are involved in formative discipline, because no believer ever should stop growing in his or her Christian life.

"Reformative discipline," I said as I continued to review, "is the work of the church when one of its members gives evidence of failing to met his or her obligations as a member of that congregations. It is the attempt of the church to hold its members accountable and responsible for the commitment made when they united with the church."

For the remainder of the evening I set before them the purpose and dangers of church discipline.

First, I listed the two primary purposes of discipline as follows, and then we discussed them.

1. <u>The first primary purpose of church discipline</u> is to help
   the one disciplined, whether the need is to awaken one to
   responsibility or to restore one to fellowship with Christ
   and the church.

   This first primary purpose must always be remembered,
   lest discipline becomes little more than harsh, prideful
   correction by a group of Pharisaical believers. We do
   not practice discipline to prove we are right and they are
   wrong, or to exalt us and humble them, but to help them
   become what Christ wants them to be in Him.

2. <u>The second primary purpose of church discipline</u> is
   to keep the church pure as God has intended and
   commanded so He may be glorified on this earth.

   This second primary purpose of church discipline must
   be seen on an equal plane of importance as the first.
   God's purpose is to glorify Himself through His church.
   He is glorified as the church is true to Him and His
   Word, as the church mirrors His purity and holiness.
   Failure to keep the church pure brings discredit to God
   on this earth and brings to His name great shame in the
   failure of those who profess to know Him.

Then I simply listed other reasons and purposes for
practicing church discipline.

1. <u>The Bible teaches it</u>--to practice church discipline is a
   matter of obeying our Lord while failure to discipline
   is a matter of disobedience.

2. <u>The preservation of the results of evangelism demand
   it</u>. What good is it to evangelize if we make no effort
   to teach and train and disciple those converts?
   Further, if new converts are dumped into an impure
   church with no godliness and commitment, what do
   we expect them to become from that example?

3. <u>The teaching of self-discipline in the life of a believer demands it</u>. Self-discipline is not something we teach ourselves, but rather it is something imposed upon us from outside of us. In this undisciplined world it is essential that the church be concerned to teach its members self-discipline, a painful lesson, perhaps, but so necessary for all aspects of the life, especially the Christian life.

4. <u>The on-going work of sanctification demands it</u>.

5. <u>The following necessities demand it</u>.

   a. to keep the church with a proper and Biblical sense of evil in a wicked world.

   b. to keep a Biblical witness before a lost world.

   c. to keep false professors from having a false assurance of a false salvation.

   d. to keep the church in unity and strength.

   e. to express the true love of the church.

   f. to prevent scandal to the outside world.

   g. to allow the church to deny the right of membership to some.

   h. to keep the church clearly identified as a New Testament church.

   i. to keep the church from becoming a house of Satan

Before we closed I set before them some dangers and abuses possible in seeking to practice church discipline. I warned them that the presence of these could do at times as much damage as no discipline in a church.

1. <u>Pride</u>--the work of discipline must be done with a humble heart.

2. <u>Legalism</u>--the work of discipline is not just a set of rules which are mechanically and coldly applied so we can say we have been faithful to the keeping of the rules.

3. <u>Extremism</u>--the work of discipline does not lead us to the place where we play Holy Spirit or God in one's life, whereby we want to make their decisions for them.

4. <u>Undisciplined discipline</u>--the work of discipline must be structured and clearly principled, and the principles must be applied fairly and consistently in each case and from one case to another.

5. <u>Arbitrariness</u>--the work of discipline must be based on Scripture not only as to how it is to be done, but also concerning matters for which one is to be disciplined, and not on matters of someone or several persons' arbitrary choice.

6. <u>Supremacy</u>--the work of discipline must not be seen to be the church's supreme and only work, but rather it is part of the necessary work the church is always engaged in.

7. <u>Asceticism</u>--the work of discipline must never be seen as an end and goal unto itself or as a means which by itself can produce spirituality and growth.

As we closed, Conrad Spratt, the chairman, made a very perceptive statement.

He said, "I can see why many churches do not practice discipline. This is a spiritual work open to many pitfalls and errors. Many churches are not spiritual enough to do the task. Let's pray, men, that we are."

CHAPTER 21

WHERE ARE THOSE WHO
HAVE NOT BOWED TO BAAL?

Be thou faithful unto death,
and I will give you a crown of life.
Revelation 2:10

The next day was Sunday, and tension continued to fill the air as we made our way to church for the Sunday School hour. I was hoping the opposition class had disbanded, but no such blessing was ours this day. In fact, the class was larger than ever and none of them seemed to want to speak to the rest of the church body.

Those who had been voted out of the church were present, plus quite a number of others. In fact they may have had as large or larger a crowd as the whole church combined. When Sunday School was over, none of them stayed for church. They all hit the exits and departed. I supposed they went home.

The next week they showed their darkened hearts even more than previously. We answered the phone dozens of times to find no one on the line, or to hear vulgar and profane words, or to be cursed.

Someone, perhaps one of the opposition, got into the information concerning my long distance calls at the telephone company, and sent me a xeroxed copy of it with certain calls circled in red and a note accusing me of making personal calls on the church phone.

One day we found a dead kitten on the front porch and another one on the back porch with the following note attached:

We hate preachers
Who act like rats.
All such preachers,
Take note of these cats.

I shuddered and almost got sick as I buried those little animals, and thought to myself, they not only hate innocent preachers, but also innocent animals.

The whole situation was beginning to get to Terry and me. It was impossible to rest or relax in our own home, not knowing what to expect next. It was even difficult to sleep at nights, and to be honest, we both slept spasmodically during this time.

One day as I was there alone a very suspicious girl came to the door and knocked. I had begun the practice of looking out through the drapes to determine who was calling before I opened the door. The reason she was suspicious looking was because she was dressed like a street-walker. Terry was not home, so I decided I had better not answer the door. When no one came to the door, she walked away and moved into the yard and out to the street only to be picked up at the curb by a car full of some of the teen-age boys of the opposition group. I am not sure what they had in mind if I had opened the door, but it sent me a warning that Garth Duncan was right--they would stop at nothing to remove me from the church.

I also began to notice that almost everywhere in town I was treated with disdain, even by people I didn't know. Some members of other Baptist churches even chewed me out blaming me for the trouble at First Baptist Church, showing they had no understanding whatsoever of the spiritual problem or battle which engulfed us. Their churches were probably just like ours before God began to work to bring purity, and they couldn't understand what God was doing any more than the opposition party in our church.

It was the loneliest time of my life. I began to understand the cost of a faithful ministry, such as that which Jeremiah had rendered for the Lord. I began to marvel how we extol these great men of God of the past who suffered so much for the truth, and even the great men of church history who suffered so much also, but somehow we have a closed mind to the possibility that one could suffer in the same manner today standing for the truth.

Everything is more important than truth in our day. Career is more important than truth. Peace is more important than truth. Money and salary are more important than truth. Reputation is more important than truth. Advancement in the denomination is more important than truth. Unity at any cost is more important than truth. A larger church is more important than truth.

Where are the Jeremiahs of our day? Where are the Elijahs, the Martin Luthers, the Pauls, and others who heard and followed the words of Jesus concerning self-denial and sacrifice? Where are those who will leave father, mother, brother, son or daughter to be His disciple? Where are those who would be that grain of wheat who would fall into the ground and die that they might bring forth fruit for eternity?

Could it be that we have more in common today with the Cains, the Baalims, the Korahs, the Demases, and the Judases than we do with the Moseses and the Christs?

I fought against developing a martyr's spirit such as Elijah had when he fled from Jezebel, or a negativism as possessed by John the Baptist when he was in prison.

Many a night I laym awake praying and thinking of such matters, fighting feelings of despair and discouragement.

Where were those who had not bowed their knees to the Baals of our day?

CHRISTIAN MEN, we are not at war with any man that walks the earth. We are at war with infidelity, but the persons of infidels we love and pray for; we are at warfare with any heresy, but we have no enmity against heretics; we are opposed to, and cry war to the knife with everything that opposes God and His truth: but towards every man we would still endeavour to carry out the holy maxim, "Love your enemies, do good to them that hate you."

---C.H. Spurgeon

THE CHRISTIAN SOLDIER has no gun and no sword, for he fighteth not with men. It is with 'spiritual wickedness in high places' that he fights, and with other principalities and powers than with those that sit on thrones and hold sceptres in their hands. Some Christian men are very apt to make Christ's war a war of flesh and blood, instead of a war with wrong and spiritual wickedness. We are fighting for God and his truth against error and against sin; but not against men. Woe, woe, to the Christian who forgets this sacred canon of warfare. Touch not the persons of men, but smite their sin with a stout heart and with strong arm. Slay both the little ones and the great; let nothing be spared that is against God and his truth; but we have no war with the persons of poor mistaken men.

---C. H. Spurgeon

CHAPTER 22

WHAT ABOUT MATTHEW 18:15-18?

As many as I love I rebuke and chasten....
Revelation 3:19

As I recognized the pressure which was upon our lives and home, I tried to understand if the deacons were feeling something of the same. The Thursday and Saturday night meetings of study and prayer became more essential for our unity as the time unfolded. As far as I could tell, they were holding up under the strain.

The next Thursday evening we began working through individual passages to determine the principles they set forth on the subject of discipline. Our plan was then to follow up that study with final conclusions and a plan and program for the practice of church discipline.

That Thursday evening we were back in Matthew 18:15-18. I had studied the passage carefully so that I could guide them in the study together.

I read the passage to them to refresh their memories:

15 Moreover, if thy brother shall trespass against thee, go and tell him his fault between thee and him alone; if he shall hear thee, thou hast gained thy brother.

16 But if he will not hear thee, then take with thee one or two more, that in the mouth of two or three witnesses every word may be established.

17 And if he shall neglect to hear them, tell it unto the church; but if he neglect to hear the church, let him be unto thee as an heathen man and a publican.

18 Verily I say unto you, Whatsoever ye shall bind on earth shall be bound in heaven; and whatsoever ye shall loose on earth shall be loosed in heaven.

Next I set before them the following principles:

1. Every church member is to be interested in the work of church discipline--that is, in the work of helping and correcting a brother (or sister), especially if that sin is against him or her.

2. Every church member is given a pattern to follow in this work of church discipline as follows:

   a. <u>An admonition from one brother to another</u>
      If your brother sins against you
         go and tell him his sin
         between the two of you--alone
      If he hears you, you have gained a brother

   b. <u>An admonition from several brothers</u>
      If your brother refuses to hear you
         take one or two witnesses with you
         so every word may be established
      If your brother hears you (implied)
         you have gained a brother

   c. <u>An admonition and action by the church</u>
      If your brother refuses to hear the witnesses
         take it to the church
      If he hears the church (implied)
         you have gained a brother
      If he refuses to hear the church
         you (singular) treat him as a heathen
            that is, as a lost person
         you (singular) treat him as a publican
            that is, as a harsh, greedy, deceiver

   d. <u>An admonition grounded and backed by heaven</u>
      Whatever you (plural) bind on earth
         shall have been bound in heaven
      Whatever you (plural) loose on earth
         shall have been loosed in heaven

I realized that I needed to make some further explanation.

"This passage sets forth the simplest form of church discipline--member toward member. If the sin of member toward member cannot be worked out, the formula becomes a little more complex and involves members toward member. If the sin is not worked out from that formula, then it becomes more complex--church toward the member who is offending. If the matter cannot be resolved in that formula, then the original member who went to this brother is commanded to treat (it is a singular verb) him (the offending brother) as a heathen or publican. But it is not just the action of the offended brother alone, for the next verse, verse eighteen, makes it clear that the church has acted also as binding and loosing are plurals. These plural verbs speak of the fact that the church (not just the individual) has acted in the matter and that action is the expression of the will of God in heaven."

When the time of questions arrived, several important ones emerged.

"What sins are we talking about here?" voiced Bob Motley. "Why didn't Jesus name the sins involved here?"

"I can only suggest a possibility to answer this question. Could it be that Jesus gave no list of sins to keep the work of discipline spiritual? Can you imagine how legalistic men might become with a list? And even then, a list might not solve all the problems because some items which need discipline might not fit into a neat list one might give."

We closed our time together with a brief discussion of what was taking place around us in the life of the church. It seemed they were all weathering the storm except for one individual, Eli Melton, the funeral director. The problem in the church was hurting his business, not in the sense that people were no longer dying, but they were turning to his strongest competitor.

I had wondered who would be the first to shows signs of cracking under the severe pressure upon us.

Only be thou strong and very courageous, that thou mayest observe to do according to all the law, which Moses, my servant, commanded thee; turn not from it to the right hand or to the left, that thou mayest prosper wherever thou goest.

This book of the law shall not depart out of thy mouth, but thou shalt meditate therein day and night, that thou mayest observe to do according to all that is written therein; for then thou shalt make thy way prosperous, and then thou shalt have good success.

Have I not commanded thee? Be strong and of good courage; be not afraid, neither be thou dismayed; for the Lord thy God is with thee wherever thou goest.

---Joshua 1:7-9

CHAPTER 23

DO CHURCHES TODAY
EVER APPLY
I CORINTHIANS 5:1-5?

If you love me, keep my commandments.
John 14:15

He that hath my commandments, and keepeth them,
he it is that loveth me; and he that loveth me
shall be loved of my Father,
and I will love him, and will manifest myself to him.
John 14:21

Usually Friday evening for Terry and me was a time of relaxation and rest. We would go out for supper that night and sort of unwind from the week. With Saturday being a day of intensity because of the coming Sunday, Friday evening was special. But the next Friday evening was anything but special--it was sad and very painful.

Terry called me at the office about three o'clock in the afternoon. She was crying, and asked me to come home immediately. I couldn't possibly imagine what had happened, and of course my first question was concerning her physical condition. She assured me she was alright physically and under no threat or danger.

Driving the short distance home, I tried to figure out what could possibly be the problem. Terry was home early from her job, and she was crying. Could it be that someone at work took the church problem out on her?

When I arrived home, Terry had stopped crying, and was now facing the situation with determination and courage.

The story she told me angered me with an infuriation I had not known for a long time--even back into my pre-Christ days. She had been fired from her job because of me and the problem at First Baptist Church. It seems her boss owed a large sum of money to Garth Duncan's bank (he was the president), and part of his deal to extend the credit to Terry's company was only if she was fired.

Obviously, this wasn't stated as the reason she was fired. They had told her she was not competent at her job, which was ridiculous. She could work circles around any other secretary in the office. She was the kind of person who had a job done while others were still thinking about it and organizing it. In fact, we found out later that they had to hire two girls to take her place, she had taken on so much of a work-load. We chuckled when we heard that, but, of course, we didn't know that this sorrowful evening.

It wasn't that we couldn't get by without the money--we could. But we were trying to save some for a hoped-for future child, or even for future seminary training for me. The worst part was the humiliation of it all, and the understanding that these people could control our lives in such an unfair manner, and we had no recourse to pursue to rectify their unfairness and injustice.

Our minds wondered what these people would do next.

When Saturday evening arrived for our deacons' meeting, Eli Melton was missing. His excuse was his business, and in a way I could understand the busy time of Saturday evening for a funeral parlor director. But he had made other arrangements for the previous Saturday evenings so he could be with us. Naturally, I wondered if the pressure of the opposition had finally gotten to him in its fullness.

The passage for this evening was I Corinthians 5:1-7, an important text for the subject of church discipline. It is the account of open sin in the Corinthian church and Paul's teaching as to how the church was to deal with it.

I divided the passage into several main headings.

I   THE ABOMINATION OF ONE MAN IN THE
    CHURCH

   Fact: <u>A member of the Corinthian church was guilty of a
          deep and scandalous sin.</u>

1. It is such a deep sin that it is not even named among the Gentiles (vs 1).

   That is quite a statement--that such a sin would not be allowed to exist even among the Gentiles in Corinth, especially since the word "Corinthianize" meant to live in the most blatant sexual lawlessness and license. Yet here a man in the church at Corinth is undeniably out-corinthianizing the Corinthians in his sexual practice.

2. It is the sin of fornication of an unusual kind (vs 2).

   This man is involved with his father's wife in some immoral sexual relationship, no doubt, adultery (porneia). But there is some question as to the exact form this adultery has taken. Some expositors argue that the verb here (have) refers to the marriage relationship (Matthew 14:4, 22:28; Mark 6:18; I Corinthians 7:2, 29). Further, it could be argued that the past tense verbs here ("the one who did this work" as in verse 2 and also "the one who has done this" in verse 3) speak of marriage having taken place. Others argue that it was probably a permanent relationship (concubine or mistress) but without marriage.

   But all are agreed that it was clearly a continual association and not just one act or a relation of short duration. But this was not what made it so offensive to even the Corinthians--concubinage or adultery would not have offended them. That which was even out of bounds to them sexually was for a man to have his father's wife.

   The term "father's wife" is not certain. It could have been his mother--that would have been terribly offensive even to the heathen. Or it could have been his stepmother--that also would have been offensive. She was no doubt not even a professing Christian and surely not a member of the Corinthian church or Paul would have passed the same judgment upon her as he did the man.

3. It is a sin that is a well-established fact (vs 1).

It is not that the man has been accused, but denies it. It is not that there are suspicions yet unproven. It is not that it is a vague and uncertain rumor. Rather it is a certain, well-established, undeniable and open fact admitted by and known to all.

II THE ATTITUDE OF THOSE IN THE CHURCH

Fact: <u>The Corinthian church is proud and puffed up over the matter rather than mournful.</u>

A. The Pride Which Existed in the Church

1. They are not proud of his action.

Surely that could not be. Who could be proud of such an extreme case of adultery?

2. They are proud in that they will not admit it.

Perhaps they are like parents who have a child with a serious problem, yet they cannot bring themselves to admit that THEIR child could possibly have such a problem.

3. They are proud in that they will not deal with it.

It's much easier to hope that the problem will go away on its own. To confront it could be painful to themselves and to the members of his family.

They would then be admitting the reality of the situation in all its ugliness. Then the world would know and they could no longer deny it. How comical--the church with such a problem not even existing in the lost world.

B. The Sorrow Which Should Have Existed in the Church

1. The sorrow should have been greater than the pride.

   The use of a comparative here with the word mourn indicated their mourning should have been deeper than the height of their pride. It is not just pride contrasted with a neutrality. It is pride contrasted with deep mourning--the opposite of their attitude.

2. The sorrow must precede the correct action.

   As long as pride existed in their midst, they would take no action against this man's sin. But when they were broken in sorrow over the sin in their midst, understanding it's abominable nature before God, realizing its destructive nature in the life of this man, and acknowledging its paralyzing and corrupting nature in the church, then they would act strongly and correctly against the sin.

III THE ACTION PRESCRIBED BY PAUL TO THE CHURCH

Fact: The church must take immediate action.

A. The Necessity of the Action (vs 3)

1. Paul has already made a spiritual judgment concerning this matter as to what must be done.

2. They are to follow his instructions in the matter.

B. The Authority of the Action (vs 4)

1. They are to act in the name of the Lord Jesus,
    that is, by His authority.

    This is not something they are doing on their
    own--out of their own desires and for their
    own purposes. They are acting in His authority
    and in His behalf.

2. They are to act by His power.

    No human being has the power to do what Paul
    commands. But because God has commanded it,
    we do it by His power.

C. The Content of the Action (vss 4-5)

1. The action is to be taken by the church as it
    gathers together (vs 4).

    This is not the action of the elders or the deacons
    alone. This is the action of the church as a body.

2. They are to turn the offender over to Satan for the
    destruction of the flesh (vs 5).

    There is some question as to what the phrase
    "destruction of the flesh" means. Some have
    interpreted it to mean to turn him over the Satan
    so he can kill him. But there is another
    possibility--that it means to turn him over to
    Satan so he may destroy his carnal and fleshly
    lusts and attitudes in this area of his sin. The
    word "flesh" does at times refer to the sinful
    nature of man (Matthew 26:41; Romans 6:19,
    8:3, 7:5, 8:8-9; II Peter 2:18; I John 2:16,
    Galatians 3:3; 6:8).

Could this not refer to God allowing Satan to afflict him, even bodily, to bring his lusts and fleshly appetites in check? Did not Paul speak of his own bodily affliction as coming from the messenger of Satan (II Corinthians 12:7)? Was not the minister of Satan sent to Paul to keep him from pride and exaltation above measure because of the abundance of revelation given him?

Thus, though these are not exactly the same, it is still the messenger of Satan having a spiritual result in men to humble and break them that they might praise and glorify God all the more. And is not this the need of the offender at Corinth? He is puffed up in pride and in dire need of a breaking and humbling. His fleshly desires and nature needs discipline. The means proposed by Paul is to turn him over to Satan for bodily affliction which God would use to remedy him of his sin and bring him back to Himself.

Though not mentioned specifically, the action, because of its extreme sinfulness, also would include excommunication from the fellowship of the church until the dealing of God was finished in him. Then restoration to the church and it's fellowship would follow.

I had gone somewhat longer in our study than usual. We closed by noting that we were not aware of anyone who was committing such a blatant sin in our midst, but if ever there was such a case, we must be willing to act as commanded in the Scriptures.

However, there were several lessons for us to note for church discipline in general.

1. The church is to have a concern for the lives of its members.

2. The church is not to ignore sin in its midst.

3. The church is to sorrow when one of its members falls away.

4. The church must not fear to act when necessary in the dealing with the sin of its members.

5. The church must practice various kinds of discipline for different kinds of sin.

6. The most severe sin is worthy of the most severe action of turning one over to the devil for the destruction of the flesh.

7. The Lord will honor the church's action and He will use the negative act of Satan against the man to bring spiritual good and restoration to the man, as painful as it may be.

The next-to-last question of the evening was if any of us had ever heard of a church doing such a thing?

The answer was no.

The last question was if any of us knew a church of our day ever practicing any kind of reformative discipline.

Again, the answer was no.

Conrad Spratt closed in prayer, commenting that it is no wonder our churches are so powerless and weak.

My final comment was, "Yes, and no one wants to pay the price to bring the church back to her purity and power."

CHAPTER 24

WHO CAN HELP ME NOW?

Why standest thou afar off, O Lord?
Why hidest thou thyself in times of trouble?
Psalms 10:1

The following Sunday had been the original deadline the opposition group had given me for resigning the church. I didn't know quite what to expect as we got up that morning and got ready to go to church, especially in light of the dirty work they had done the previous week.

They did gather for their Sunday School class, but they took care of more than Sunday School that day, as I found out just after our church service. None of the opposition group had stayed, but Garth bolted into my office after the services as I was preparing to head home for Sunday dinner.

He was very demanding and authoritative as he spoke.

"Mr. Pointer!" he said rather formally.

At least he had stopped addressing me as pastor.

He continued in the same authoritative manner.

"We met this morning in business session and it is now concluded that our group is the First Baptist Church of Collegetown. We took official action to vote you and your followers out of the membership of the church. We determined that your action of a few weeks ago whereby you sought to vote us out was illegal and therefore not binding. We will give you and your group one month to vacate the building and turn all the papers, funds, and properties over to us. We are prepared to give you three months salary, which I think is more than a fair compensation to you. Are there any questions?"

"What if we refuse to recognize your action?" I asked.

"We will take whatever action is necessary to get you out and to repossess this building!" he replied rather matter of factly, as if he was speaking of taking a Sunday afternoon walk.

"Any action necessary?" I queried.

"Any action!" he offered with confidence.

"Sinful action?" I asked further.

He was quiet.

"Violent action?" I pressed him further.

Silence again filled the room.

"Unchristian and unbiblical action?" I shot at him again.

Again, no reply.

"Unbaptistic action?" I asked pushing him even harder.

Silence.

"Garth," I challenged him, "how can you live with yourself doing what you have done already? How can you look at yourself in the mirror in light of the unchristian, unbiblical and unbaptistic actions you are involved in?"

"We have only done what we had to do. This is our church and no one is going to take it away from us," he fired back.

"No, Garth!" I retorted. "This is not your church nor is it my church. It is the Lord's church, and we have an obligation to order the affairs of this church not according to my desires or your preferences, but according to the Word of God. If any man develops the attitude that it is his church, and fights against the Lord to get his way against the Lord's way, that man is placing himself in a very dangerous position."

"Are you threatening me?" he barked.

"No, I am not threatening you. If I would have done as I wanted to do I would have beaten the tar out of you a long time ago. I would have thrown you and your little group out of this church bodily long ago. But I am not free to act as I wish. I must act in accordance with His Word. Yes, I must and do love you, but I cannot compromise with your wishes to continue the impurity of this church. There are Biblical standards which must be upheld. I invite you to repent and to disband your group and to come and help us build a godly and spiritual body of people here. How can you sanction the lives the people with you are living? Do you live that kind of life also, Garth? Is it that you know that if judgment of sin begins in this church, your sins will have to go? Is it that you are comfortable in your sins and refuse to turn from them? You profess to know the Lord, but to be honest with you, Garth, I have never seen any evidence of salvation in your life since I have been here as pastor. Could it be that you are not saved and that if you were to die this moment you would be in hell separated from God for all of eternity."

That did it. He bolted from the room in a rage.

He spouted as he went out the door, "Be out of here in a month!"

I didn't have much appetite for Sunday dinner that day. We were a sad lot, Terry and I, with neither one of us saying anything. We sort of sat and played with the food on our plate.

Finally, I spoke.

"Well, do you still feel like you did that morning in the hospital after they beat me up? Do you still feel it's worth the fight?"

She smiled faintly and said, "Well, I guess I need to make another trip through the Psalms, don't I?"

It wasn't a very happy service Sunday evening, either. All the deacons were there except Eli Melton again.

As I drifted off to sleep that evening, I knew it would not be a pleasant week either. I had to go see Eli and encourage him in the battle. I wondered how much encouragement a defeated general could give to one of his captains.

Again my thoughts turned to Lime Creek Baptist. I found myself envying my old buddy Todd Shelton. He had followed me as pastor there.

I remembered the days of great revival there--souls saved in great number.

I remembered the unity of the church--hardly a problem in the days I spent there.

I relived all the events since I had come here to First Baptist Church.

Maybe I was at fault. Maybe I was too stringent. Maybe I was unloving. Maybe I had come on too strong. Maybe I had even made a mistake in coming here. Maybe I should leave. Maybe I should go on and finish school.

Maybe...! Maybe...! Maybe...! There were dozens of them.

The dark hour of the soul had come and I had no physical nor spiritual strength left with which to fight. Terry was even worn and broken.

Who could help me now?

I got out of bed and read the following verses:

I mourn in my complaint, and make a noise because of the voice of the enemy, because of the oppression of the wicked, for they cast iniquity upon me, and in wrath they hate me. My heart is sore pained within me; and the terrors of death are fallen upon me. Fearfulness and trembling are come upon me, and horror hath overwhelmed me. And I said, Oh that I had wings like a dove! for then would I fly away, and be at rest. Lo, then would I wander far off and remain in the wilderness. I would hasten my escape from the windy storm and tempest.
                                                    Psalm 55:2-8

Save me, O God, for the waters are come in unto my soul. I sink in deep mire, where there is no standing: I am come into deep water, where the floods overflow me. I am weary of my crying: my throat is dried: my eyes fail while I wait for my God. They that hate me without a cause are more than the hairs of my head: they that would destroy me, being my enemies wrongfully, are mighty.
                                                    Psalm 69:1-4

Lord, how are they increased that trouble me! Many are they that rise up against me. Many there be who say of my soul, there is no help for him in God.
                                                    Psalm 3:1-2

I prayed with tears, weeping with heavy and consuming sobs. All I could say was, "Lord, that describes me. Help me!"

CHAPTER 25

PASTOR, CAN YOU COME OVER RIGHT NOW?

Help us, O Lord our God;
for we rest on thee, and in thy name we go against this multitude.
O Lord, thou art God; let not man prevail against thee.

II Chronicles 14:11

Finally that Sunday night I slept--so deep I hardly heard the phone ring about midnight. I tried to clear my head as I answered it.

I blurted into the phone a not-too-conscious, "Hello!"

The voice at the other end spoke in staccato fashion, "Pastor, can you come over right now?"

Staccato fashion or not, I recognized the voice was Eli Melton.

Still trying to clear my head and shocked to hear from Eli, I froze for a few seconds.

"Pastor? Are you there?"

"Uh, yeah, I guess so. I was asleep."

"Can you come over right now?" he repeated.

I heard voices in the background, and knowing Eli and his wife lived alone, I asked, "Eli, where are you?"

For a few seconds there was no answer. Not only was Eli silent, but the voices in the background went dead also.

Then he spoke.

"Uh, I'm alone at home."

"Eli, who's with you?" I asked

"What difference does it make?" he snapped. "Can you come over right away?"

I tried to explain.

"Eli, you call me late at night and say you have to see me. Evidently you want to talk about something important. But you are not alone as you call. Doesn't that raise the question of whether you are calling on your own or if someone has put you up to it?"

His response was quick and to the point.

"Preacher, I'll call you tomorrow!"

Then he hung up and left me standing in the dark half-awake and half-asleep wishing he had never called to begin with.

Immediately, though, I dialed his home, but no answer. Either he refused to answer, figuring it was me, or he was not home. Wherever he was, he was with a group of people. My curiosity peaked wondering who they were--members of the opposition party, perhaps?

I didn't sleep much that night, noting that it is difficult to go back to sleep once one has been roused from a deep sleep. When you go back to bed the mind becomes hyper-active, and one can say good-bye to any sleep.

I awakened the next morning knowing that I had to call Eli (that is, I awakened, if I slept at all). When I did he agreed to meet me for breakfast.

Before anyone could even take our order, he launched into an explanation of the past evening.

"Pastor, I'm sorry to call you as I did last night. It was my only option."

He then unravelled a story of how Garth Duncan and several members of the opposition party had come by his house last night to pressure him to unite with their cause.

"Preacher, I couldn't get them to leave. They were making such accusations against you and against the deacons. I told them you needed to be there to answer their accusations. They laughed and said you didn't scare them. They stayed on and on. They were bound and determined to get us to join them. You talk about pressure--boy, they applied it. They threatened my business--said they were going to take over the church whatever it cost."

He was talking fast by now, which was unusual for Eli, being a smooth-talking and calm funeral director.

"It was then," he continued, "that I figured my only hope to get them to leave was to call you and have you come over. They hate you and don't even want to be in the same room with you. They're afraid of you. So I called you, and only then did they promise to leave. So then I told you I didn't need you to come over. I know it was confusing to you, but that's the story.

"Do you know, preacher," he went on unable to stop because he was so worked up, "that they are going to see everyone in the church and pressure them just like they did me. They're not going to leave one stone unturned. They mean business!"

I figured it was my turn to speak so I did.

"Well, the question I am most interested in, Eli, is whether or not they swayed you? It appeared to me that even before they arrived, you were beginning to buckle a little bit."

"You're right, preacher," he admitted. "I must say I was discouraged. I missed last Saturday night's Bible study with the deacons because of that. But I must also admit that the Word you have preached here and taught us has done something to my life. I for so many years didn't know much Scripture. Oh, I believed the Bible, but no one ever really taught us what it says or how it applies to our lives. Now I can't turn back. I must carry on following the truth of Scripture wherever it might lead."

"Even if it costs you business?" I asked.

He paused a few moments then replied honestly, "Even if it costs me my business. Even if it costs me my life!"

I went from breakfast back to church. I praised the Lord that He never lets his servants down--even in their discouragement. He had sent just what I needed that morning. The renewed commitment of Eli had spoken to my heart. Eli didn't know it but he had been more of a blessing to me that morning than I could ever be to him. I was convinced the Lord would sustain the remnant. He was with us. He was leading and teaching us. He would not forsake us.

When I got to the church, my old buddy Todd Shelton was waiting to see me. I hadn't seen him or talked to him since the wedding, which is unusual. Usually we talked ever two weeks or so.

Kiddingly he greeted me, "Boy, it must be nice being pastor of a First Baptist Church."

O Thou of little faith,
   God hath not failed thee yet!
When all looks dark and gloomy,
   Thou dost so soon forget--

Forget that He has led thee,
   And gently cleared the way;
On clouds has poured His sunshine,
   And turned thy night to day.

And if He's helped thee hitherto,
   He will not fail thee now;
How it must wound His loving heart
   To see thy anxious brow!

Oh! doubt not any longer,
   To Him commit thy way,
Whom in the past thou trusted,
   And is 'just the same today.'

---Selected

CHAPTER 26

A PREACHER CAN'T DO NOBODY
NO HARM, CAN HE?

The glory of the Lord appeared in the cloud.
Exodus 16:10

There are times when the enemy in his fury overdoes his work, and instead of the results he desires, he gets the opposite. Such was, it seems, the case as the opposition worked so strongly against us. Their bold and aggressive actions only entrenched the people of God with a stronger determination to stand for the truth.

Even the young converts, whom I had feared would be damaged by the turmoil, were growing. Troy and Bonnie Medford continued to advance in the faith and the knowledge of the Word. Barton Medford was a strong witness to the whole family. They could not deny the change which had taken place in his life, but then that became a point of dislike and misunderstanding of the enemy also.

"Poor Barton and Troy and Bonnie," they said. "They have been hoodwinked by that young preacher. He's got some kind of demonic power over their minds and lives."

Troy's problem, the one which led to his conversion, was still in limbo, even after these several weeks had passed. He continued under suspension from police duty until the investigation was over. We were praying about the matter continually. But nothing seemed to surface that would clear him. Troy and I met once a week for discipleship, at which time I also encouraged him concerning the situation.

It was on the Monday afternoon following the "down" Sunday when Troy called me. His voice was excited but subdued on the phone.

"I think I have a lead on the absent gun," he informed me.

I was more excited, at least outwardly, than he was.

"What's going on?" I asked.

"I had a phone call from out of the blue this evening," he offered. "It was from a known informant who said he had some information for me. He was a guy who owed me one from about a year ago."

"Well, what is the lead he gave you?" I quizzed him eagerly.

"I haven't talked with him yet. I'm supposed to see him this evening at 8:30."

"Do you have someone going with you?"

"No, not yet."

I offered to accompany him if he desired.

He turned me down at first saying it could be dangerous.

I laughed and replied, "It might be the safest place in town as far as my life and health are concerned in Collegetown."

Troy picked me up in his car at the church at 7:45. We prayed for safety and for the profitability of the trip for Troy's case. It wasn't a long drive, but he didn't want to be late--a man after my own heart.

We drove into one of the slum sections of town, and stopped about half a block down from a dingy restaurant-type of bar. Nearly-connected houses dotted the streets on both sides. It was dark and there wasn't much activity on the street. A few people passed by headed somewhere, because none of them lagged or dallied.

No one was hanging out on the street, so it appeared there was no danger. But there were a lot of dark pockets and shadows up and down the street where someone might hide.

"Where's he supposed to meet us?" I asked eagerly.

"He'll find us," Troy answered in an official police-type tone of voice. He then unlocked both of the back doors.

Troy's professional eyes scanned the street ahead, the houses across the street, and even the area behind us. He appeared calm and cool. My heart was pounding.

I thought its no wonder this church trouble doesn't phase Troy. He faces tense situations constantly.

Then Troy spotted him.

"There he is," he whispered without moving his head.

His eyes sharpened. I couldn't see much of anything.

But then as I watched a figure emerged from the shadows of an alley. He walked briskly towards us. When he got along side of us he stopped for a split second, scanned the streets and the houses, and then jumped in the back seat. Troy started the car and pulled away from the curb.

Our passenger stayed low in the back seat and he and Troy began a conversation.

"What have you got for me, Dink?"

"Hey, I thought you would come in alone," he protested, referring to me.

"This is my preacher!" Troy replied. "You can trust him. He's an okay guy."

"Yo' preacha?" Dink echoed in something of a mocking form. "I guess a preacha can't do nobody no harm, can he?" he laughed.

"I got yo' word that you ain't never gonna tell where you got this, ain't I?" he begged .

"You sure do, Dink!" Troy guaranteed.

He passed something over the seat to Troy. It was wrapped in a piece of cloth. As Troy drove, he unwrapped it. It was a gun.

"That's the gun he pulled on you!" Dink said.

"How do I prove that?" Troy asked.

"He said before he died he ain't got no gun, don't he?" Dink explained.

Troy nodded.

"His friends say he ain't got no gun, don't they? Well that's his gun--got his name on it!" Dink clarified.

"Yes, but all this gun proves is that he was a liar--he owned a gun when he said he did not. It does not prove he had it at the scene of the crime nor that he pulled it on me," Troy reasoned with him.

"Who do ya think picked up that gun and ran off with it?" Dink offered with pride.

"You mean you were there?" Troy asked in near unbelief. "I thought we got all his friends."

"You never get the Dink!" he chortled with a brassy air.

"But I still don't get it." Troy puzzled. "How do I prove he pulled this gun on me?"

"Go dig his bullet out of the telephone pole behind you." he suggested.

"His bullet? But he didn't fire at me."

"Yes he did, big police man," Dink motored on obviously enjoying himself. "The two of you musta' fired bout the same time, and so it sounded like only one shot. You knew you shot but you never know he shot. Dig that big bad bullet out and you got you some proof of your story. Just don't squeal on me. None of those other boys know who picked up that gun. Fact, they dunno what happen to it. They may not even know he let one go at you."

We let him out of the car at a designated corner and he disappeared into the darkness.

Troy was silent as we drove home. Then he let out a subdued "Praise the Lord. I think we've got what we need to clear me, if we can only find that bullet."

Back in front of my house we prayed together before I got out. We even prayed for Dink, along with prayers of thanksgiving.

Troy thanked me for going, and I assured him it had been my privilege to help him.

It had been a long and blessed Monday after a difficult and draining Sunday. I crawled into bed exhausted, shared the marvelous story with Terry, and then I was gone.

What a difference one day makes! In the lowest depths of despair on Sunday night and now on the mountain tops on Monday night.

It was a lesson not to live the Christian life on the basis of feeling and emotion, but of the need to praise God for all His dealings with us as we are assured of His sovereign control over us and all the events surrounding us.

The next day I had to laugh as I replayed the incident. Dink was still on my mind, especialy his words, about a preacher not being able to do anybody any harm. How men are prone to look at a Christian's human power and not to the supernatural power available to him. Maybe that's why they think they can do us such great harm with impunity.

CHAPTER 27

WHAT ABOUT GALATIANS 6:1?

*The Lord hath his way in the whirlwind and in the strom,
and the clouds are the dust of his feet.
Nahum 1:3*

As the week unfolded before me, I tried to think of something to do to thwart the opposition's demand and threat that we vacate the building and recognize them as First Baptist Church within a month--or else.

I had thought about calling the police and shutting them out from the use of the building for their unauthorized Sunday School class on Sunday morning, but had ruled that out on several grounds. It would have exposed the conflict even in a greater way to the lost community, which I did not think was beneficial to the cause of Christ. I could visualize the opposition before the television cameras and and radio talk show microphones telling their sordid and twisted story. Such action might also have stirred the fire of the conflict to violent proportions whereby someone might get hurt, which I did not want to see.

I was shut up to the Lord and His working to resolve the issue in His manner. If He wanted us to continue as a witness for Him in Collegetown, He would have to move in our behalf and show us the way.

The opposition, I knew also, was busy campaigning to get people on their side and to turn out for the big meeting following their month deadline to us. We did not campaign, except at the throne of God through prayer. He was our hope and power--not the methods and tactics which depend on man. We were shut up to Him.

The study of church discipline did continue, though I began to wonder why we continued. There seemed to be no way we could ever be able to apply such discipline in our setting. But the study did give the deacons an understanding of why we were in the mess we were--because of the church's neglect of Biblical discipline for so many years. It also gave them a conviction that we were right in what we were doing.

Thus we continued to meet on Thursday and Saturday evenings. The next Thursday evening we considered Galatians 6:1.

> *Brethren, if a man be overtaken in a fault, ye who are spiritual restore such an one in the spirit of meekness, considering thyself, lest thou also be tempted.*

I then set the content of the passage before them as follows:

I   THE MAN WHO HAS SINNED

A. <u>He is a believer</u>.

Though the text does not call him a believer, but only refers to him as a man (anthropos), the context indicates clearly he is a Christian.

B. <u>He is a member of the local congregation</u>.

Again, this is not stated, but the context of the book, as it is written to local churches with doctrine and practical application of that doctrine in the church, indicates such.

C. <u>He has been overtaken by a sin</u>.

The whole scenario is hypothetical, but nonetheless, the brother in the illustration has fallen into sin. We are not told what sin or what sort of sin it is. Greater stress is placed on how he came into this sin by both the verb and the noun used for sin.

The verb indicates he was taken by surprise by the sin--it came upon him unexpectedly. The noun used for sin speaks of a stumbling aside, or a false step, or a lapse, or a deviation from the truth or righteousness. This is not to excuse his sin or to play it down in its seriousness, but it does not seem to be a blatant rebellious attitude about sin which we saw in I Corinthians 5. The man has fallen into this sin and seems to be crushed in his attitude about it, not denying or minimizing its seriousness.

Thus the key difference between the two cases (this one as contrasted with I Corinthians 5) is the attitude of the offender. He needs encouragement and application of the grace of the gospel rather than condemnation and the shock of excommunication. There seems to be a potentially repentant heart if only the promise of forgiveness of the gospel can be communicated to him.

II THE MEN WHO ARE TO RESTORE HIM

A. The spiritual men of the church have a responsibility toward him.

The task of discipline, whether it be positive or negative, must be handled by the spiritual men of the church. Probably this is the most spiritual work a church ever does. All spiritual work requires spiritual men. The most spiritual of spiritual work obviously even more so requires spiritual men to do it. Any others trying to do this most spiritual task will surely make a total wreck of it.

Who are these most spiritual men? Would they not be the elders or deacons? Do not the qualifications stated for them in I Timothy 3 set them apart as the most spiritual of the church?

B. The spiritual men of the church have a responsibility to seek to restore him.

The word restore does indicate that his sin has had
some serious effect on him and his relationship to the
Lord and possibly the church. The sin has knocked
him from his spiritual walk, from his relationship
and fellowship with the Lord, and from his
commitment and active life in the church. There is
some mending to be done to bring him back into the
right way where he once was.

There is no question of his salvation here--that is
assumed as a fact. He probably has shown clearly in
the past that he is a true believer. Even now his
attitude is not that of indifference and unconcern as
he lives in an unchristian life style as do many who
are church members. Rather his former state is
undeniably that of a Christian, and now what is
needed is restoration to that former state.

C. The spiritual men of the church have a responsibility
   to seek to restore him with a proper attitude.

   The attitude they are to possess is that of meekness,
   that is, with a mildness, a kindness, a forbearance or
   a gentleness. This does not speak of a weakness or
   vacillating attitude. This work must always be done
   with a firmness, but it must be a firmness with a
   gentle, loving spirit. How easy it is to drift to either
   of the extremes when disciplining--either a bold
   insensitive harshness or a mushy backboneless
   compassion.

D. The spiritual men of the church have a responsibility
   to seek to restore him with special concern for their
   own lives.

   The spirit of meekness is necessary, lest the one
   doing the work of restoration himself be tempted. It
   could be that if one seeks to do the work of
   restoration without meekness, but rather does the
   work with pride, as if to say he could never fall into

sin himself, that the Lord might allow him to face severe temptation to humble him in attitude and heart. Thus the unsympathetic brother learns sympathy by the severity of temptation and even by falling into sin himself.

It could also be that this is a warning that one who is doing the work of restoration needs to keep his heart before the Lord, lest as he is forced to think upon his brother's sin (his temptation and fall into it and the actual sin itself), Satan might gain a foothold to trip him into sin.   In simple words the brother involved in restoration will have to allow into his mind thoughts of sin and its practice that he ordinarily would not be contemplating. Surely the sorrow he sees in his brother is a message of warning against imitating the brother in his sin, but Satan is such a liar that if one is not on guard he could find his sinful appetite or lust for sin stirred to practice it. The danger is that the lust would take over, and in many cases when that happens the sinful human heart fails to weigh or denies to itself the final consequences which would follow with its exposure.

Following this presentation, I summarized some of the key points the passage taught concerning discipline.

1. The church has a definite responsibility to see the restoration of one of its members when sin has invaded to break that one's fellowship with the Lord.

2. The church has a responsibility to do the work of restoration by the power of the Holy Spirit.

3. The church as it seeks to do the work of restoration by the power of the Holy Spirit, therefore, has the responsibility to give the work of restoration into the hands of the most spiritual among them, no doubt the elders and/or deacons.

4. The church has the responsibility to do the work of
    restoration with the attitude of humility and meekness.

5. The church, if it practices the work of restoration with
    the wrong attitude, may do great harm to the one they
    are seeking to restore or possibly even to the ones doing
    the work of restoration.

As we ended, we prayed for the proper attitude as we
sought to do the work of discipline. How much different it
would have been were we to be dealing with just one
person, rather than hundreds. We concluded that the work
of discipline, if neglected, becomes a seeming impossibility.
It was like allowing a child to grow up without any
formative or reformative teaching, and then when he is
twenty-five to try to correct him. He has become a spoiled
brat.

Was that not what our church was spiritually? A group
of spoiled unspiritual brats? And were not their actions now
against us only the temper tantrums of uncontrollable and
undisciplined monsters? What do you do with such when
the day of opportunity to discipline has passed? Can it be
anything except the church becoming incorrigible and
hopeless to correct unless God intervene?

CHAPTER 28

WHY CAN'T WE WORK
A COMPROMISE?

Man shall not live by bread alone,
but by every word that proceedeth out of the mouth of God.
Matthew 4:4

The next morning I headed for the church a little later than usual. I had to take Terry to a new job. The Lord had been gracious in opening another door for her, and this was her first day at work. It had the appearance of being even a better job than the previous one.

When I did arrive at church, there was a visitor waiting for me. It was Garth Duncan. I was amazed at the man's boldness in coming around when he was involved in such rebellion against me and the church.

He greeted me in a very friendly manner, which aroused my suspicions to the hilt.

"Good morning, preacher! I've got an offer to make to you today."

It reminded me that many people want to run the church like a business. You wheel and deal, not caring who you step on or what rules you break. If you can get your own way, so much the better. If you can't, then you threaten, bluff and stonewall. If you win that way, so much the better also. But if you can't win by these tactics, then suggest a compromise. At least you will get part of what you want, if not all. In the compromise stack the deck in your favor and hope your opponent buys it. Never give in unless you absolutely have to and only as a last resort.

He followed me into my office almost uninvited. He took a chair and not even waiting for me to sit down, he took off.

"I want to suggest a compromise that will save all of us a lot of heartache," he began.

I said nothing, and I'm sure he read my suspicious face.

"We will call off this whole matter on certain conditions," he continued, evidently hoping to get at least the response of a request to know the conditions.

I said nothing again.

"If your group will accept our group back into the membership and fellowship of the church, and if your group will include three or four of our men on the deacon board, we will come back and call off the ultimatum and action we plan to take to regain our church."

I noted he still used the phrase "our church" indicating he had not changed his mind about the issues.

"Garth, you want to talk about conditions? We have some conditions too," I challenged.

He warmed up thinking we were now moving in the direction of negotiations and a settlement.

"Alright, state your conditions," he said in a business-like tone.

"We will accept you all back on the condition that you are all Christians--that's the first condition," I informed him.

"Sure, we're all Christians. That's no problem," he offered, thinking the first condition was an easy one.

"Wait just a minute, Garth," I cautioned. "You gave me your testimony a week or so ago, and your testimony of what a Christian is was not a Biblical one. You set before me a way of salvation by works. You said nothing about Christ, faith, grace and about the Bible. You said much about Garth and his works as your hope of spending eternity with God."

He began to make excuse.

"So I'm not a theologian! I've been a church member for years. I've taught Sunday School. I've been a deacon. I was treasurer for a number of years. I've given thousands of dollars to the church. Doesn't that count for something?"

"Garth, that's just the point. Listen to what you are saying! Where is Christ in your testimony. Where is the knowledge and conviction of sin? Where is the grace of God to an undeserving sinner? Where is faith in the person and work of Christ as the only hope of a wretched sinner? Your testimony shows that you do not understand salvation. Therefore, how could you be a Christian?"

He was speechless. I wondered if the Lord was speaking to him. I continued.

"If you and those with you will bow to the Lord Jesus Christ as sinners to receive the payment He made for your sin, He will not only save you, but He will also grant you the understanding to see that what you have been doing the past several weeks is totally against His will and Word. You will be sorry for your actions, and you will then apologize to the church and we will then begin a program to teach and train you in the Word of God and you will be considered for church membership."

His response was purely business-like again.

"Oh, don't play hardball with me, preacher. We've got the pitch and clout to knock you out of the batter's box and send you to the showers. You're talking to the man who has out-hardballed all the best in this town. You can't bluff me."

"Garth, that's part of your problem. You see this as a power play and you expect that if you get the upper hand, we will buckle. Let me inform you that we're not playing hardball or softball. We're playing Bible-ball. We're doing what we're doing because of a commitment to the truth and authority of the Bible. We don't come together every time you rattle your glove and sneer at us with your threats to try to decide what to do next in some game of strategy. We have been doing what we were convinced was taught in the Bible and we will continue to do the same regardless of what happens. No matter how much strength you appear to have against us, no matter how many numbers of people you rally around you, no matter how much pressure you put upon us, we are going to walk the same road--the pathway spelled out for us in the Word of God."

"You mean there is no compromise?" he demanded in amazement.

"No compromise!" I affirmed.

"You mean there can be no negotiations?" he said in bewilderment.

"Read my lips, Garth. No compromise, no negotiations, no deals, no changes in our position, no giving in to pressure. If it were a matter of insignificant concerns, like where to put the piano in the church, or what color shall we paint the wall, we would negotiate and work out some compromise. But this is far more serious than that. This concerns the nature of the gospel and the doctrine of salvation. This concerns His church, whether it will be the pure body He demands or whether it will be filled with worldlings. On these matters there can be no compromise."

He was absolutely flabbergasted!

"Well, I never..." and he never finished the sentence. He walked out in another rage.

I could hope that he would leave my office only to have the Spirit of God convict his heart and bring him true repentance, and for this I did pray.

Yet I also realized the other alternative was that he would give himself more completely to opposing us than before.

CHAPTER 29

WHAT ABOUT THE FALSE TEACHER OF I TIMOTHY 6:3-5?

Be not afraid nor dismayed by reason of this great multitude;
for the battle is not yours, but God's.
II Chronicles 20:15

After Garth had left, I turned to study the passage I would consider with the deacons the next evening. As I went through it, I marvelled at the Lord's providence--it spoke rather clearly of what I had just gone through with Garth--the importance of doctrine and the necessity of the church to discipline those who are denying the truth.

The passage was II Timothy 6:3-5. It reads as follows:

> *3) If any man teach otherwise, and consent not to wholesome words, even the words of our Lord Jesus Christ, and to the doctrine which is according to godliness,*
> *4) He is proud, knowing nothing, but doting about questions and strifes of words, of which cometh envy, strife, railings, evil surmisings,*
> *5) Perverse disputings of men of corrupt minds, and destitute of the truth, supposing that gain is godliness; from such withdraw thyself.*

I constructed the following outline for the next evening:

I   THE CHURCH HAS A CLEAR STATEMENT OF DOCTRINE IT MUST UPHOLD

Fact: The church has a clear doctrinal standard and it is not difficult to determine.

Fact: <u>The church, having a clear doctrinal standard, can
            also determine false doctrine which is not in
            agreement with it</u>

   1. It is doctrine foreign to Christianity (vs 3).

       Literally the Greek terms it as "teaching other
       doctrine."

   2. It is unsound doctrine (vs 3).

       Again, literally the one spoken of here is not
       assenting to sound, wholesome or uncorrupted
       doctrine. He is holding unsound doctrine.

   3. It is the doctrine which disagrees with that of
       our Lord Jesus Christ (vs 3).

       Again, literally the one spoken of here is not
       assenting to the doctrines of our Lord Jesus
       Christ.

   4. It is doctrine which does not promote godliness
       (vs 3).

       Literally, again, the one spoken of here is not
       assenting to doctrine which promotes godliness.

II THE CHURCH HAS A CLEAR STATEMENT OF A
FALSE TEACHER WHO HOLDS FALSE DOCTRINE

Fact: <u>The false teacher is vividly described and
            censured</u>.

   1. He is puffed up with pride.

       The pride here is no doubt his enthroning his
       own convictions in place of the authoritative
       doctrine of Christ and the church. Literally, he
       has been demented with conceit. This is a perfect

tense verb, indicating this puffing up with pride was something which took place in the past, but still exists today. He has crowned himself as the final authority and argues from that basis even now, instead of bowing to the authority of Christ and God.

2. He knows nothing.

   Literally, he is now at the present time unable to comprehend anything of the truth. His understanding is twisted and warped because of a refusal to bow to the authority of God.

3. He centers on the unimportant.

   Correct doctrine to him is not important. He has a fondness and obsession for unprofitable and trivial matters of controversy.

4. He stirs up all kinds of sin.

   Out of his concern for the unimportant, or even out of his lack of concern for the important comes many problems to the church. Only the truth produces a godly life. His falsehood, because it conflicts with the truth, will stir dissension, for even falsehood is convinced of its position and of the importance of it, while being incapable of seeing the truth and its importance. Obviously, you can never expect one who holds to falsehood to stand for the truth. And such a one will never understand the one who holds the truth being willing to stake his life and his all upon it, even making it a life and death point of contention.

   Therefore, when the one holding falsehood is allowed to spread it in the church, envy, strife, railings, evil surmisings and perverse disputings

will follow. There will always be such when the
truth collides with error. The only way there
cannot be such attitudes and sin present is for one
of the two sides to compromise or concede. And
is it not strange that the one standing for the truth
is always the one who is expected by others to
compromise, and when he doesn't he is the one
who is blamed for the trouble and division?
The one holding the truth is labelled as narrow
and dogmatic, while the false teacher and his
followers are seen as those longing for unity and
harmony. The one holding the truth is asked to
give up and change his position, but who ever
asks the real troublemaker, the one denying the
truth, to give up his position?

These false teachers are so deceived and destitute
of the truth that they suppose that gain according
to worldly standard (money, size, numbers, etc.)
are the sign of God's blessings. They are blind
to the real evidences of God's blessings--the
spiritual standards as seen in the life of Christ
and His apostles.

III THE CHURCH HAS A CLEAR STATEMENT OF ITS
RESPONSIBILITY TO RID THE CHURCH OF THE
FALSE TEACHER

Fact: The church must withdraw from such a false
        teacher (vs 5).

1.   This is a command that comes for Timothy.

     The statement of the command to withdraw from
     such a person comes to the individual, Timothy,
     who is a leader or elder of the church. He is to
     withdraw fellowship from this one. He is to
     refuse to recognize him as a true teacher of the
     Word of God. He is to refuse to have fellowship
     with such a person.

2. This is a command that by implication also belongs to the local church.

   If the elder of the church is to treat a false teacher in this manner, it would be absurd to think the local church can treat such a one in any different manner. It would make some sense, if we did not have the Scriptural teaching here, for the local church to withdraw fellowship, but the elder would be allowed to fellowship with him to seek to help him. But it makes no sense at all to command the elders, who are strong and sound in doctrine, to withdraw from such a one, and then allow the members of the local church, who are not as established in true doctrine, to fellowship with and hear him.

   So clearly, the command to the elder is to be taken as a command for the congregation also.

When we met on Saturday evening, I also shared my conversation with Garth Duncan with the deacons. It was amazing to them also how Garth fit the description in our passage.

I went home that evening rejoicing, but also realizing that one week of the ultimatum was past, and three more weeks remained. We were moving into the early part of March. By early April the matter would be settled, unless the Lord wanted to settle it sooner.

Blessed are you, when men shall revile you, and persecute you, and shall say all manner of evil against you falsely, for my sake. Rejoice and be exceedingly glad; for great is your reward in heaven; for so persecuted they the prophets who were before you.

---Matthew 5:11-12

But beware of men; for they will deliver you up to the councils, and they will scourge you in their synagogues.

---Matthew 10:19

And you shall be hated of all men for my name's sake, but he that endureth to the end shall be saved.

---Matthew 10:22

The Son of man came eating and drinking, and they say, Behold a man gluttonous, and a winebibber, a friend of publicans and sinners.

---Matthew 11:19

Then the Pharisees went out, and held a council against him, how they might destroy him.

---Matthew 12:14

And when they had called the apostles, and beaten them, they commanded that they should not speak in the name of Jesus, and let them go. And they departed from the presence of the council, rejoicing that they were counted worthy to suffer shame for his name.

---Acts 5:40-41

CHAPTER 30

DID YOU KNOW YOU'RE MARRIED TO A HERETIC?

Are you he that troubleth Israel?
I King 18:17

As I got up the next morning, a Sunday, I began preparing myself for whatever might happen. Who could predict what the opposition had in store? And especially since they did much of their dirty work on Sunday. And since I had clashed with Garth only Friday, I wondered what they might pull today.

But if I was surprised when the day unfolded with nothing happening, I was not disappointed. I gave a sigh of relief when the day was over, and figured we might have a few days relief from the threat of the opposition. But I was wrong!

On Monday morning I attended our local Baptist denominational meeting, a business session made up of representatives from all the churches. As I walked in and sat down in the back, I noticed Garth Duncan was present. He had never in the months since I was pastor at First Baptist attended such an event. I began to feel heavy of heart as I tried to imagine what he had in mind.

When the time of new business arrived, which followed all the reports and planned stuff, Garth was the first to jump to his feet.

"I am here representing the majority of the members of First Baptist Church. Our pastor is in conflict with us, and we have tried everything to resolve the issue. However, he is young and stubborn and will not even consider suggestions of compromise which we have made. We have tried to negotiate a peaceful settlement, but all we have done has fallen on deaf ears. A certain minority of the church has followed him with a blind loyalty. We honestly do not know what hold he has over them.

"We do hate to take the following action, but we have concluded it is the only possibility open to us. We are not acting on our own. We have sought the best, highest and most reliable counsel possible in our Baptist denomination, both at the local and state level.

"Therefore with reluctance and sadness of heart, yet convinced of the necessity to save the church for our denomination, we are bringing heresy charges against the pastor, Ira Pointer. He is doctrinally unsound, and he is not an Evangelistic Baptist as evidenced in his church practices. At the proper time we will state in detail the content of these accusations, but for now we put the matter on the floor of our local Baptist association, and ask your help in resolving this matter of examining him and judging him in his beliefs and actions. Thank you."

The moderator didn't quite know what to do with this motion. I don't think the association had ever considered heresy charges against anyone, even though we had pastors in our group who denied the inspiration of Scripture, the virgin birth of Christ, the bodily resurrection, and other central planks of the historical Baptist doctrinal system.

Someone seconded the motion (I think it was one of the opposition party again), and then the moderator tried to dodge the bullet.

"I see the man who is accused, Brother Pointer, is present today. I wonder if he would like to speak to the motion?" he suggested.

I realized that I faced an impossible task if I were to try to address the group. How do you tell them all that had happened in the past weeks?--the lies, the hatred, the unchristian actions, the disregard of Baptist polity, the rebellion in refusing to listen to the authority of the church, the threats, the renegade Sunday School class, etc. and etc. Could anyone believe it if I even had or took the time to tell them?

I tried to make it short but not necessarily sweet.

"Mr. Moderator. Thank you for the opportunity to speak. I would like to point out to you that this motion is out of order because the one bringing it, Mr. Garth Duncan, is no longer a member in good standing in one of the churches of our local association, let alone being a representative of one of the churches. Therefore, clearly he has no right or privilege to make such a motion. Whether his accusations are right or wrong, and I surely would dispute them, his motion is definitely out of order, and I call upon you to rule it as such."

Again the moderator was stumped.

The local associational worker came to his defense.

"Mr. Moderator. Whether Mr. Duncan and his group are members of the First Baptist Church or not is part of the disagreement of this dispute. One side says they are and one side says they are not. Therefore, I don't think you can rule this motion out of order on the stated grounds of Mr. Pointer. That would be to rule the motion out of order not on a clear and undisputed premise, but on one that is the heart of the dispute--surely not a fair action."

I rose to speak again.

"Is it not true that only representatives of this executive group can make motions? If so, is not this motion out of order on that ground?"

Again the moderator was in a bind.

Again the denominational worker rose to his defense

"Is it not also obvious that Mr. Duncan could not be a representative of Mr. Pointer's group, seeing they have voted him out of the church? In fact, Mr. Duncan's group, which also claims to represent the First Baptist Church, has voted him as their representative. I think it would only be fair to receive both of these men as representatives until the dispute is settled and we can then receive one and reject the other."

Someone made a motion to that effect, and the motion was passed. So the motion to bring heresy charges against me was legally and officially now back on the floor.

Someone then made a motion that the matter be sent to the proper committee to deal with it and then bring a report back to the executive body as a whole.

I rose to speak again.

"I want it clearly understood that these charges are being brought against me and not against First Baptist Church. It is not the right of the committee which will hear the charges to decide which group is the First Baptist Church, for that would be to meddle in local church affairs, which is definitely against Baptist polity. Neither you nor your associational worker has any authority to interfere, dictate, or judge the matters of a local church. Neither does the committee to which you send this motion.

"You can censure me as a heretic. You can censure the First Baptist Church as holding heretical doctrines. You can deny us membership and representation in this body of Baptists, but you cannot tell us which of these two groups is the First Baptist Church.

"These people represented by Garth Duncan requested in a regular business meeting of the First Baptist Church that their names be removed from the membership roll of the church. This was done.

"There is absolutely no question about it--they are not members of the First Baptist Church of Collegetown. Your recognizing them as having some ground to claim to be the church is absolutely unfounded in principle and ungrounded in Baptist polity.

"Again, I say, you can censure me and you can censure the local church I pastor. You can, if you so desire deny us representation in this body. But you cannot force the First Baptist Church to receive this group back as members. Neither can you make them the First Baptist Church. We have a First Baptist Church of Collegetown, and they are the ones who make all the decisions regarding that local church. Any attempt by this association or any of its representatives or employees to do otherwise is a severe breach of Baptist polity, in which case this association had better investigate itself to determine if it is still a Baptist organization. I am fearful that already there are grounds to question the actions of some within this body to that effect."

After a little more wrangling by some of those who speak, it seems, to hear their own voices, those who say a lot but say nothing, the matter came to a vote.

It passed--which meant that now I was officially on trial before the appropriate committee of the local Baptist organization of our denomination for heresy!

Wait till I tell Terry that she's married to a heretic!

CHAPTER 31

HOW CAN WE POSSIBLY BE A PURE CHURCH?

Be ye not unequally yoked together with unbelievers; for what
fellowship hath righteousness with unrighteousness? And what
communion hath light with darkness?
II Corinthians 6:14

The next day following the heresy motion, the phone in my office rang off the hook. Suddenly everyone wanted to know what was going on over there at First Baptist Church. I never knew I had so many preacher friends. Either that or many of them were pure curiosity seekers. All acted as if they would support us, but then I remembered that none of them said a word the previous day when the motion was being debated.

There was one phone call worthy of note. It was one of the members of the committee before whom I would be charged. He was the former associational worker in our area who had retired a year or so previously. In fact, he was the chairman of the committee. He had not been able to attend the previous day's proceedings, but had read the minutes and he boldly told me I was absolutely right in what I had pointed out to the representatives present. In fact, he was outraged that the matter had even been referred to his committee.

"What you are experiencing over there at First Baptist Church is strictly a local church matter. If you need our help, you call us--we don't call you. That's the principle we ought to be following."

I just about fell over backwards in my tilting desk chair. I had never heard a denominational man talk like that.

He continued.

"And the idea you're a heretic is ridiculous. Why this association hasn't had a heresy trial in its history, and it has been over fifty years since even a local church disciplined anyone. Now all of a sudden we're going after you. And for what? Because you believe and preach the Bible and want a pure church. It's atrocious!"

I rejoicingly replied, "Brother Jones, you're my kind of Baptist!"

"Yes!" he said, "And we're both Evangelistic Baptists! Don't worry about the trial, son. It's not going to get to first base."

I thanked him for calling, and then realized I had reached a conclusion from the conversation, and it was not one about the heresy charges. It was one about denominational workers. I concluded that there are good pastors and bad pastors. There are good church members and bad ones. And there are good denominational workers and bad ones.

Just because a man is a pastor does not mean he is all he claims to be. Just because one is a church member doesn't mean he or she is all that one claims to be. And just because one is a denominational worker does not mean that one is all he claims to be.

But on the other hand, just because there are pastors who fall below the standard you might expect, that does not mean they all do. Just because some church members fall beneath the standard expected does not mean they all do. And just because a few denominational workers fall below the standard does not mean they all do.

There is nothing that makes one all he should be automatically just because he becomes a pastor, a church member or a denominational worker. I must not allow myself to get down on denominational workers or our denomination just because one or two individuals over-stepped their boundaries in serving the churches.

The date of the trial was set for a week from that day--a Tuesday.

The Thursday evening deacons' study presented us with another challenging Scripture, II Thessalonians 3:6.

Now we command you, brethren, in the name of our Lord Jesus Christ, that ye withdraw yourselves from every brother that walketh disorderly and not after the tradition which he received of us.

I divided and presented the verse as follows:

I   THE CHURCH IS GIVEN A COMMAND

A. <u>It is a command from Paul</u>.

Yes, the command comes from Paul and it is a command--an imperative.

B. <u>It is a command to the church</u>.

Paul addresses them as brethren as he writes the church at Thessalonica.

C. <u>It is an authoritative command</u>.

Obviously, all commands from Paul are authoritative as he held the office of an apostle. Yet this one is given further weight and obligation because it comes to the church in the name of the Lord Jesus Christ.

II   THE CHURCH IS GIVEN A COMMAND TO WITHDRAW FELLOWSHIP FROM CERTAIN BROTHERS

A. <u>The command is to withdraw fellowship</u>.

The verb itself here speaks of withdrawal, avoiding, shunning or abstaining from familiar fellowship. When the verb is followed by the Greek preposition <u>apo</u> it gives it greater weight, stressing separation from.

Thus the action here is a withdrawal of fellowship. Certainly, in order for the members of a church to do this there must be a determination of wrong-doing and an announcement of the necessary action towards the brother.

B. <u>The command is to withdraw fellowship for disorderly conduct</u>.

The disorderly conduct here speaks literally of the one walking about in contradiction to the prescribed conduct or out of rank with the requirements of Christ and His Word.

The Scripture is full of the requirements for the walk of a Christian;

1. We are to walk in newness of life (Rom. 6:4).
2. We are to walk after the Spirit (Rom. 8:4).
3. We are to walk in honesty (Rom. 13:13).
4. We are to walk by faith (II Cor. 5:7).
5. We are to walk in good works (Eph. 2:10)
6. We are to walk in love (Eph. 5:2)
7. We are to walk in wisdom (Col. 4:5).
8. We are to walk in truth (II Jn. 4).
9. We are to walk in the commands of our Lord (II Jn. 6).
10. We are to walk not after the flesh (Rom. 8:4).
11. We are to walk not after the manner of men (I Cor 3:3).
12. We are to walk not in craftiness (II Cor. 4:2)
13. We are to walk in humility of mind (Eph. 4:17).

Surely, we are not suggesting these all be taken as a literal straight jacket to be placed on each person to determine if there be some deviation--just one. No, rather do they not give us a clear description of the general trend of life expected of a Christian? And should not a Christian's life fall into this pattern? And if and when it does not, is there not a serious problem which must be recognized by the church?

Restoration is desired and proper, if possible, but if not the church must act in the discipline of withdrawal for the warning and benefit of the person and also for the purifying of the church.

C. <u>The command is to withdraw fellowship for not
    walking after the teaching they had received</u>.

   Whereas the first command to walk not disorderly
   speaks of morals and practices, this second seems to
   speak of doctrinal matters, though some take it to
   speak of walking practically after the commands of
   the apostles and Christ.

   Whatever the case, there is a prescribed walk for the
   believer. He is not free to walk any way he wishes.
   He is one who is under authority and obligation to be
   what he committed to be in the acceptance of the truth
   and substance of teaching he received at salvation.

When I finished the presentation of this passage, Conrad
Spratt said, "Isn't it time to withdraw fellowship from all
those following the opposition? They are walking disorderly
and not after the substance of the Biblical teaching."

I must confess I did agree. But how could we do it?
How do you purify such a corrupt church where the lost out-
number the saved?

Surely the Lord had an answer as to how we could be a
pure church! But right now, I didn't have it.

And He spoke this parable unto certain who trusted in themselves that they were righteous, and despised others:

Two men went up into the temple to pray; the one a Pharisee, and the other a publican.

The Pharisee stood and prayed thus with himself, God, I thank thee that I am not as other men are, extortioners, unjust, adulterers, or even as this publican.

I fast twice in the week; I give tithes of all that I possess.

And the publican, standing afar off, would not lift up so much as his eyes unto heaven, but smote upon his breast, saying, God be merciful to me a sinner.

I tell you this man went down to his house justified rather than the other; for everyone that exalteth himself shall be abased; and he that humbleth himself shall be exalted.

---Luke 18:10-14

CHAPTER 32

CAN WE BRING OUR GUNS
TO CHURCH?

I came not to call the righteous but sinners to repentance.
Luke 5:32

I spent much of the following days preparing for my trial. I sought to anticipate every charge they might bring against me, and how I would answer it. I thought about not showing up as a protest of the injustice and impropriety of the trial even being allowed to take place, but I decided against that action. Some might interpret such an absence as an admission of guilt.

On Friday I got a call from Troy which I thought would be about his situation with the police department. Part of it was--his charges would be dealt with on Monday. He asked me if I would attend. I agreed, and then realized I would be attending two trials in two days--his on Monday and mine on Tuesday.

But that wasn't the only reason he called. He wanted to tell me Dink was in the hospital. He told me he had met secretly with Dink a second time, and had shared the gospel with him. Then Dink had called several times with questions about becoming a Christian.

"What happened to put him in the hospital?" I asked.

"Oh, he got in a fight with the wrong fellow--some guy about 6 foot 5. Poor Dink never had a chance being only 5 foot 6," Troy said with a slight chuckle.

"Is he badly hurt?" I asked.

"No, probably just an overnight case. But he wants to see you!"

I couldn't imagine why Dink would want to see me. I had said little or nothing when I met him with Troy in the dark streets of town. He had commented that preachers couldn't harm anybody. He didn't seem to have much knowledge or respect for me beyond that.

Thus it was with some uncertainty and hesitation that I made my way to the hospital. When I walked into the room, he was quite friendly.

"Hey, my preacha friend, Mr. Ira," he blurted out almost with glee to think I would visit him.

I had planned something of a speech to lead him to the presentation of the gospel, but no speech was needed.

"Hey, man, I think I need to accept this Jesus fellow Troy has told me about. I sure need something, or I'm going to wind up in the grave and in hell."

I thought, "What a contrast! Miss Lilly accused me of telling her she might go to hell if she didn't repent and she got bent all out of shape about it--when I didn't even say that. Now this tough street guy tells me he is going to hell if he doesn't repent."

We talked for an hour or so about the gospel--its meaning and implications. I didn't want to push him to do something which he did not understand or which he was using only as some passing fancy because of an emotional reaction to some trouble he was in.

At the end of our visit, he asked if he could pray and become a Christian. I cautioned him again about the seriousness of the hour, and went over once more the facts of the gospel. At the end of the conversation, he committed his life to Christ and I left him rejoicing over the grace of God to a lost and hopeless sinner.

His last statement was, "Preacha, I'm gonna be there Sunday, and I'm gonna bring a crowd of my friends. Get us a row or two ready in your church! We gonna help you in your battle against the bad guys tryin' to throw you out."

I assured him we would welcome all those he would bring, but that we must allow the Lord to fight the battle for us. I wondered where he had gotten his information concerning the church problem. I laughed as I thought of what Garth Duncan and his friends would say if and when they saw Dink and his buddies turn out to worship with us. I could imagine the false accusations.

When I got back to my office, I called Troy to share with him the news. He had already heard--Dink had called him to share his new joy. I asked Troy if he would work with Dink to disciple him, but he told me they had already planned to do that.

As I sat in my office following the phone call, I couldn't help but spend some time in prayer thanking God for the lost souls He had brought to himself even in the difficulty of the days we had faced. Troy and Bonnie Medford, Barton Medford, and now Dink--all saved and giving evidence of truly knowing Christ. And they all had been saved even knowing the trouble in the church.

My meditations were interrupted by a phone call from Dink.

"Preacha, I hope you don't mind my callin' you."

"No, Dink, I'm always glad to hear from you. What can I do for you?"

"Well, Mr. Preacha, I been readin' this Bible in my room, and I'd like for you to pick up one somewhere for me, when you can. I want a Bible of my own. I'll be glad to pay you for it, but I sure would like to have one."

I thought to myself, I wonder how he intends to pay for it--I hoped not with stolen money. I assured him I would get him one and it would be my gift to him.

Then he asked several more questions.

"Do me and my buddies have to wear suits on Sunday? Some of them may not have one."

I assured them that suits were not a must to come to church on Sunday.

His last question raised some real possibilities.

"What about the weapons? Most of these guys have some blades and even guns. I ain't sure I could get them to leave them back."

I replied best I could.

"Well, Dink, obviously we would rather not have any weapons at the church, and I am sure you understand that. But we don't have any metal detector at the door of the church and we have never searched anyone before letting them into the services of the church. Do your best to discourage them from bringing them into the church."

To be honest, and I hated to admit it, but I would feel safer with Dink and his friends at this point than I would with Garth and his friends--weapons or no weapons.

Oh! how great a work it is to gospelize any man, and to gospelize a poor man. What does it mean? It means to make him like the gospel. Now the gospel is holy, just, and true, and loving, and honest, and benevolent, and kind, and gracious. So, then, to gospelize a man is to make a rogue honest, to make a harlot modest, to make a profane man serious, to make a grasping man liberal, to make a covetous man benevolent, to make a drunken man sober, to make the untruthful man truthful, to make the unkind man loving, to make the hater the lover of his species, and, in a word, to gospelize a man is, in his outward character, to bring him into such a condition that he labours to carry out the command of Christ, "Love thy God with all thy heart, and they neighbor as thyself."

Gospelizing, furthermore, has something to do with an inner principle; gospelizing a man means saving him from hell and making him a heavenly character; it means blotting out his sins, writing a new name upon his heart--the new name of God. It means bringing him to know his election, to put his trust in Christ, to renounce his sins, and his good works, too, and to trust solely and wholly upon Jesus Christ as his Redeemer.

Oh what a blessed thing it is to be gospelized! How many of you have been gospelized? I contend for this, that to gospelize a man is the greatest miracle in the world.

---C.H. Spurgeon

CHAPTER 33

WHAT HAVE WE IN
II THESSALONIANS 3:14-15?

Through thy precepts I get understanding;
therefore, I hate every false way.
Psalms 119:104

The Saturday evening session was upon us again with a rapidity that made it difficult to keep up with the study necessary. Our passage for this evening was again in II Thessalonians--chapter 3 and verses 14-15.

14) And if any man obey not our word by this epistle, note that man, and have no company with him, that he may be ashamed.
15) Yet count him not as an enemy, but admonish him as a brother.

Again, I set before them the content in a study outline form.

I   THE NECESSITY TO HEAR THE WORD OF GOD AND OBEY IT

The necessity is put in the form of a conditional clause stating a hypothetical case in a negative form.

A. There is the possibility one may not hear.

Actually, the Greek word used here means more than just hear without reference to action. Rather, it means to obey what is heard, or to submit to what is heard in one's life.

The possibility stated in this verse is that one may not hear with a heart to obey or to submit to what is heard.

B. <u>There is a possibility one may not hear the Word</u>.

The point of contention here is not whether one hears the ideas of men and obeys, nor the thought of the church and submits, but whether one hears the Word of God and responds with obedience. The Word of God in the text is represented by the reference to Paul's epistle--no doubt, the one he has just finished. But because of Paul's apostolic authority, it is the Word of God. Thus the admonition can carry in its application to the whole of Scripture.

II THERE IS THE NECESSITY TO DISCIPLINE SUCH A ONE WHO REFUSES TO HEAR THE WORD

A. <u>The church is to take note of such a person</u>.

The word means to mark or beware of. Here the command is to the church as it is plural. Obviously if this is to be done, the church must have a concern and an awareness of how its members are living. Are the members obeying the Word of God, or are they living in disobedience to the Word? Any church member who says it is his business how he lives and that it is no one else's, including the church's--that one is unscriptural in his perspective and argument.

B. <u>The church is to take note and is not to keep company with such a person</u>.

Obviously, this is the action of the church to withdraw its fellowship again from such disobedient persons. The command is not to mix or mingle with that person, not to have familiar fellowship with that person, not to have intimate friendship with that one.

C. <u>The church disciplines such a person in this manner to cause him to be ashamed and repent</u>.

The danger to the member who is never reminded of his sin or disciplined by the church is that he will allow his life to drift on in that state of disobedience. We will feel no shame or sorrow. He will justify his sin and failure, if he recognizes it, by various means. He may be convicted, but not enough to bring him back to faithfulness and obedience.

But when the church disciplines him in the above manner, his sin will be pointed out. He will, it is hoped, feel shame for it as he realizes he has failed the Lord and he knows others realize it also. If he doesn't come to shame, his heart will be hardened, but at least his sin has been pointed out, and many times even from that perspective of hardening, God works.

D. <u>The church disciplines such a person treating him as a brother and not as an enemy</u>.

We have seen in some earlier cases of discipline that the church is to treat the offender as a lost person. Here the admonition is to not treat him as an enemy or adversary, but as a brother. The difference is the severity of the sin.

It may be that in the passing of time, if the brother hardens his heart and continues in his sin, or if he reacts very negatively to the church's discipline, that the church will have to treat him as a lost person. But at this point he is to be treated as a brother in Christ.

E. <u>The church disciplines such a person admonishing him as a brother</u>.

The word for admonish means to warn. Warn him of the potential seriousness of his state unless he returns to the life and commitment he once knew. Warn him of the chastening hand of God as he

works in the lives of his children. Warn him of the
effects of his present life of unconcern on his family
and others around him.

When we had finished our discussion of the passage, I
told the men what to expect the next morning at church--how
God had saved Dink and he was bringing his friends.

They were full of questions, and I sought to answer
them all.

How would these people dress?

How will they act?

Will there be various races present with them?

What will you preach on?

What will Garth Duncan and his group think?

Is this a one time thing or will they be back?

What do we do if there is trouble?

When I finally got home, I realized something else.
With Dink thinking of membership we would move out of
the pattern of family perpetuation of the church--only
members of the families already on the membership roll
making professions of faith in Christ.

I realized that such a movement was truly Scriptural.

CHAPTER 34

WHO ARE THESE PEOPLE?

The Spirit of the Lord is upon me,
because he hath anointed me to preach the gospel to the poor;
he hath sent me to heal the brokenhearted,
to preach deliverance to the captives,
and recovering of sight to the blind,
to set at liberty them that are bruised.
Luke 4:18

Sunday morning dawned with uncertainty rising with the sun. What would happen with the opposition today? What would happen with Dink's group today? What would happen if Garth and Dink's group collided? How would our faithful sixty accept Dink and his group?

It was a fairly normal (normal in comparison with the past several weeks) during the Sunday School hour. The opposition group met for their Sunday School class, even adding a few more people. They had about eighty adults. The regular Sunday School met also as normal.

But it was towards the end of the Sunday School, about twenty minutes before the morning preaching service, that Dink and his group showed up. I thought perhaps in talking with him that previous week that he was just winding, and that he might not even materialize. But, lo and behold, there they were in the parking lot of the church. And they were a motley crew to behold--all races and kinds of people--about twenty-five of them.

When this unique group walked through the doors of the church, and even passed Garth and his people in the halls, I wished I could have seen his face. The ushers told me he was livid. He stood for several minutes speechless and watched them go into the sanctuary.

Then he asked one of the ushers, "Who are these people? What does that preacher think he is up to? The nerve of that guy--bringing trash like this into our church! What's he trying to do, scare us?"

Evidently, he was so disturbed and curious about it that he stayed for the church service--the first time in weeks.

I preached an evangelistic message that morning, switching from my usual passage of exposition. Dink and his group behaved quite well. And I didn't see any guns or knives! And our people welcomed them heartily.

But not everyone was happy with their attendance, I found out after the service. When I got to my office again, there was Garth, just boiling.

"Preacher, don't think you can scare us off!" he warned.

I said, "Garth, I have no idea what you're talking about."

"You know what you're up to and so do we," he barked back. "The deadline Sunday is one week off, and suddenly those thugs and dregs of society show up, and you expect us to believe all that is normal? Ha! We're not that stupid. I'll bet you even paid them to attend to try to scare us!"

I wanted to say several things. The time was ripe for a sarcastic answer.

I could have said, "Yep, and we told them to be sure and bring their guns and knives. Didn't you see them, Garth? Why one of those guys is even a murderer!"

For all I knew, one of them might be a murderer. But there was no need to stir Garth further about the matter. I tried to calm him down by assuring him they were there of their own accord and I had no idea whether they would be back next Sunday or not.

He left again in another rage, as usual. It seems that's the way he always goes out of my office. But as he opened the door, he almost knocked Dink to the ground. He had come to the office to see me, and had waited until I was finished.

"Do you want that I should go after him and teach him some manners?" Dink asked.

"No, Dink, we need to pray for him. As Christians we don't fight our own battles. The Lord fights for us."

"Yeah, preacha, seems like I read the other night where Jesus said something like that," he remembered. "He told us to love the bad guys and pray for them. And then that Paul said to heap coals'a fire on their heads. I had a hard time figuring that one out. It sounded pretty good at first, then I realized it must mean to be so good to him that he is ashamed of his actions."

It was obvious he had been reading somebody's Bible. I complimented him on his knowledge of the Bible for one who hadn't been a Christian very long.

Then I reached back on my shelf and pulled down a Bible I had gotten him.

"Here, Dink, this is for you," I said.

"Wow, my own Bible!" he remarked, almost crying.

"Dink, this book is more powerful than your knife...."

"Oh, I ain't got no knife on me now," he said, interrupting me.

"It's more powerful than a gun..."

"Preacha, I ain't got no gun no more," he interrupted again. "Now, some of the boys outside might have one, but I ain't got mine no more."

"Well, this book is all you need now. It will tell you about the true God of this universe who is all powerful, and His power is available to us."

We chatted for a few more moments, and then he parted with his final promise.

"Preacha, I'll be here Wednesday, but I ain't sure the boys will be--but they said they want to come back next Sunday morning. So we'll be here to back you up if the bad guys give you any trouble."

I thanked him, but suggested that it might be best if we trusted the Lord to defend us, no matter what the opposition might do.

He admitted rather humorously, "Yep, you're right, preacha. If He can't do it, ain't no gun or knife going to be able to do it."

Over dinner I shared with Terry my conversations with Garth and with Dink. We laughed together, a rejoicing laugh, as we marvelled at Dink's open and sincere simplicity concerning the things of the Lord. He had more spiritual perception than Garth Duncan. We prayed for both of them.

It is a serious reflection for the evangelist, that wherever God's Spirit is at work, there Satan is sure to be busy. We must remember and ever be prepared for this. The enemy of Christ and the enemy of souls is always on the watch, always hovering about to see what he can do, either to hinder or corrupt the work of the gospel. This need not terrify or even discourage the workman; but it is well to bear it in mind and be watchful. Satan will leave no stone unturned to mar or hinder the blessed work of God's Spirit. He has proved himself the ceaseless, vigilant enemy of that work, from the days of Eden down to the present moment.

---C. H. Mackintosh

CHAPTER 35

WHO GAVE YOU THE GUN?

For I am not ashamed of the gospel of Christ;
for it is the power of God unto salvation to everyone that believeth;
to the Jew first, and also to the Gentile.
Romans 1:16

Whosoever believeth on him shall not be ashamed.
Romans 10:11

And he spoke boldly in the name of the Lord Jesus.
Acts 9:29

The next day was the day for Troy Medford's hearing. It began at 9:30 in the morning and we hoped would be over by noon. Since Troy seemed to want me there, I attended, hoping it would be over early as projected.

The investigating committee gave its report in full. It was a bullet from Troy's gun which had killed the boy during the robbery, but the boy had fired also. The gun Dink had given us was presented for the judging panel to examine. Also the spent bullet, which had been dug out of the telephone pole behind Troy, was presented. That bullet was from the boy's gun, so the investigating committee suggested that any possible case against Troy be dropped.

The ruling panel was about to rule in Troy's favor, it seemed, when the question was raised by the boy's lawyer why the gun had not been found at the scene of the crime. The explanation was given that an informant had passed the gun on to Officer Medford.

Then another question came. Who was the informant? Why wasn't he here to testify as to how he had gotten the gun, and how the gun was removed from the crime scene?

Explanation was given that Officer Medford had given his word that the informant's name would be confidential. This didn't seem to be good enough for some in the procedure. They insisted that before the panel made a ruling that the full details of the matter known to Officer Medford be disclosed. That way there would be no question of the decision as it would be made in light of full and complete information instead of the partial amount of information now possessed.

But Troy refused to give the information--he had given his word. Stern admonishment and threats followed his refusal, but he wouldn't budge. He had given his word, and that settled the issue.

When it seemed they might discipline Troy, and maybe even rule against him for his refusal to cooperate fully (as they termed it), a small figure rose in the room. It was Dink.

"I gave him the gun," Dink admitted.

The whole place went silent.

"Who are you?" asked the head of the panel.

"I'm the guy who picked the gun up at the scene of the crime and carried it away and kept it until I gave it to Officer Medford," Dink blurted out.

"Step forward, young man," he was instructed.

Dink stepped forward, gave his name, agreed to testify, and was sworn to tell the truth. The first question was why he had suddenly decided to speak up when originally he had requested confidence in the matter.

When Dink spoke up, it was pure Dink.

"Well, sir, I figured I had done my duty by giving this gun to Officer Medford. After all, it ain't gonna do the Dink much good to be known as a snitch. Then I met this fellow who convinced me I hadda come clean in this matter if I was gonna get along with Him and His way."

"Someone convinced you to come forward now?" the officials asked.

"Yep, He sure did."

"Can you give us his name?" the officials asked again somewhat puzzled.

"Sure can!" Dink teased them again, almost as if he was building the tension so his answer would have a greater impact.

"Well, speak up. Who was this fellow who convinced you to testify?"

Dink continued to lead them on.

"It was a fellow I hadn't ever met before till the other night. Some people say He's dead, but I assure you He ain't, cause I met Him."

By now the whole room was on the edge of their seats, and heartily agreed when Dink was ordered to give the man's name.

"Well, His name is Jesus, but He's more than a man-- He's God's Son!"

"When you met Him you decided you had to speak up? Explain!" ordered the head of the counsel.

"Well, when you come to know Him, and He's forgiven you of your sin, you ain't got nothin' to hide or to fear, and you gotta come clean. So my speaking up is part of the straightenin' up of my past for His sake."

The room buzzed, especially among his friends.

The questioning continued.

"You picked up this gun at the scene of the crime?"

"Yep, I sure did!"

"And you kept it for a time?"

"Yep, I sure did!"

"And you then met Officer Medford to give it to him?"

"Yep, I sure did!"

"And you asked him to keep your person in confidence?"

"Yep, I sure did!"

"And you will testify that this gun belonged to Alan Modat, and that he fired it at Officer Medford the night of the crime at the scene of the incident?"

"Yep, I sure will!"

He was questioned for several more minutes, then he was dismissed.

Before stepping down, he asked if he could say one more thing. He was given permission, but I'm not sure he would have, if they had known what he was going to say.

"I just want to recommend this Jesus Christ fellow to all of you. The more I get to know about Him, the more I love Him. He's good for all sinners, including judges, lawyers, and criminals."

With that he stepped down, beaming and shaking hands with everyone. I marvelled at his boldness to testify. He was not ashamed of Christ, and he didn't care what people thought about him. He probably didn't even know someone could be offended or think badly of him for what he had said or done.

All charges against Troy were dismissed and he was reinstated to serve on the police department. That was a great victory. But as great a victory, was what Dink had done, and no one had even told him of the need to do it.

CHAPTER 36

IS ULTIMATUM SUNDAY
STILL ON?

The Son of man shall be betrayed into the hand of men...
Matthew 17:22

With "ultimatum Sunday" staring us in the face during this week, we should have been staggering through the week with some fear. But though we were deeply concerned, and giving ourselves to continual prayer about the approaching day, there was too much going on to have time to worry about it.

Monday was Troy Medford's hearing. Tuesday was my heresy trial. Wednesday was regular prayer meeting night. Thursday and Saturday nights were deacon meeting nights. Perhaps the biggest event of the week was my trial or hearing, whatever you wished to call it.

On that important Tuesday I arrived early at the the local denominational office having prepared as thoroughly as I could. I had tried to anticipate every accusation they might make against me and I entered the building carrying a brief case full of duplicated materials to pass out to the committee members, if necessary.

The committee itself was made up of seven members. Six were fellow pastors, and the chairman was the former local denominational worker. Attending also was the present local denominational worker and Garth Duncan, who was bringing the charges. The meeting was a preliminary one to determine if there were grounds to take the matter further in the local denominational life.

The meeting opened with prayer--though I found it difficult to pray for such a meeting. I did pray for the Lord to expose the adversary for what he was, not for my benefit, but for the sake of our Lord and His church.

The chairman, Brother Jones, then spoke.

"Gentlemen, we are here to consider the suggestion that we have a case of heresy in our local church life. Let me make it clear. We are not trying a church, but we are considering Mr. Pointer in his practices and doctrine. There is some question in my mind as to whether this matter should ever have arisen, but I will not prejudice this committee on that matter, but will allow you to hear the accusations and make your own determination. Mr. Duncan, you may now present your accusations."

Garth rose, went to the lectern provided, and began.

"Mr. Chairman and all you honorable members of this committee. It grieves me to have to come before you today and make this presentation. I agonized over these matters for a long time. I even tried several times to talk to Mr. Pointer and reason with him and even work out some compromise, but I was always rebuffed in a very close-minded and rude manner. I assure you that coming before this committee is a last resort after we have tried every other avenue possible."

I had to admit, it sounded convincing, unless you knew the truth.

He continued his presentation.

"Also, before bringing the charges, let me assure you that I represent the vast majority of the members of First Baptist Church--hundreds as compared to less than a hundred who are supporting Mr. Pointer. If he wins this case, it is probable that those people will be lost to the Evangelistic Baptist denomination forever."

I thought, "Good tactic, Garth. Nothing impresses or scares Evangelistic Baptists like numbers. Never mind that they are lost to the denomination already because of their inactive lives and absent non-existent commitment."

I made notes as he spoke further.

"Now as to the actual charges, they fall into several categories. First there is the doctrinal category. This man is a Calvinist, and we all know that Calvinism is a cold system which not only kills evangelism and missions but also destroys the fellowship of a local church."

I wondered if Garth had any idea what a Calvinist was and where he had gotten the information that I was a Calvinist.

"Second, the outworking of his doctrine is evident in his ministerial practices. As a Calvinist he is cold in personality, not warm and friendly to the congregation. He is stern in his demands and does not understand the need to love men so they can come to know Christ and grow in their lives. He is stiff and legalistic in his relation to the church people, demanding they agree with him and that they live according to the rules he sets down. He is dogmatic in his doctrine and practice not willing to work with others. When there are disagreements he is not willing to negotiate or to compromise. You do it his way or else!"

I winced inside but gave no outward evidence of how his statements were affecting me.

He was not finished.

"He doesn't love lost souls for he seldom preaches evangelistically. Instead he preaches through Biblical books while lost people die and go to hell. He doesn't always end our services with an invitation challenging men to become Christians. We could have had many more baptisms this year if he had faithfully challenged people to know Christ and join the church."

I was wondering how much more he would have to say as he droned on and on.

"He has some strange ideas about church membership. I have talked to numerous leaders of our denomination and I have been told there are but three ways for one to be removed from the membership of an Evangelistic Baptist church--by death, by letter and by one's own personal request. Right now he is meeting with some of the deacons of the church and they are planning how they can rid the church membership roll of most of the members just so his little group will be left in control. He has already removed seventy or so of us and refuses to re-admit us."

He was about to quit when he remembered one more thing, something so new he hadn't even written it down in his notes. But little did he realize that what he said next might have been better left unsaid as far as his case against me was concerned.

"Finally, brethren, you would not believe what he pulled last Sunday. Since he could not fill the church with legitimate members or prospects, he filled the church with the dregs of society--blacks, hoodlums, criminals and people who don't even know how to dress to come to church. Our people went home scared half to death."

Finally he was finished, but tried to make a few points even as he closed.

"Thank you, Mr. Chairman and committee, for your time and consideration of these matters. I know you will evidence your great wisdom and decide on this matter to allow the First Baptist Church of Collegetown to remain as an Evangelistic Baptist witness in this town."

When he had sat down, the chairman nodded to me and said, "Rev. Pointer, the floor is yours."

I began by listing the accusations he had brought against me.

1. I am a Calvinist in doctrine.
2. I am against evangelism and missions.
3. I am dogmatic.
4. I am unloving.
5. I am uncooperative.
6. I preach through Biblical books instead of every sermon being an evangelistic message.
7. I don't give an invitation after every sermon.
8. I believe in responsible church membership and Biblical church discipline.
9. I brought a group of deep sinners to church not even considering their background, race or social standing in the community.

"Now, brethren, please understand that in all these matters we are discussing, I desire most of all to be Biblical. I admit the following: some of these accusations are true and some are false. Some are Biblical and some are not. Some are characteristics of Evangelistic Baptists and some are not.

I maintain that the accusations which are characteristic of Evangelistic Baptists are my characteristics also, and the accusations which are uncharacteristic of Evangelistic Baptists are uncharacteristic of me also. Let me take them one by one and substantiate my claims."

I began by considering the accusation of being a Calvinist.

"Mr. Duncan, can you tell me what a Calvinist is? I think it is only fair that if you and your group accuse me of being something and then state that this viewpoint carries such strong negative results and accompaniments, that you should give evidence that you understand the system of theology you refer to."

I paused to allow him to speak. He could only stammer and stutter and finally said, "Mr. Pointer, you're on trial here--not me."

I made my point to the committee again, and went even further.

"I challenge the committee, first of all, to disregard any accusation Mr. Duncan makes against me based on his statement that I am a Calvinist since he does not know what one is. And if he does not know what one is, there is no way he can possibly tell us the results and accompaniments of that system of theology.

"I challenge the committee, second of all, to understand that if you want me to take the time, I will document for you beyond doubt or question that the early Baptists of history and of our denomination were Calvinists. I can show it to you by citing the early Baptist confessions of faith or by reference to our early Baptist preachers and leaders or by both, if you so desire and request. The evidence of this point is irrefutable."

I turned to the chairman to ask his direction in this matter.

He smiled and said, "That won't be necessary, Rev. Pointer. Anyone who knows church history knows history is on your side, and furthermore, if we find you guilty of being a heretic or of not being an Evangelistic Baptist because you're a Calvinist, then this committee will have to find me guilty of those charges also."

I wanted to shake my fist in the air in rejoicing like an athlete when he had just made a great play, but I contained myself only allowing my heart inwardly to say, "Atta boy, Brother Jones."

I moved to the second accusation.

"Secondly, Mr. Duncan accuses me of not being evangelistic or mission-minded. I will answer that charge with several facts.

"Fact number one is that souls have been saved under my ministry since I have been at First Baptist Church. Troy Medford, a young policeman and his wife have come to know the Lord and are growing in Christ.

"Fact number two is that even one of my attackers (I'm sure you men have heard about my being beaten up recently) has been saved and he too is advancing in Christian life. I add here, does that appear that I am unloving towards the lost, when our love went out even to the one who beat us?

"Fact number three is that we had a church full of sinners last Sunday because God saved one of them from the depths of sin, and he had a burden to bring his friends to hear the gospel. Several of them are under conviction and we are praying for them as well."

I couldn't resist turning the tables on Garth at this point.

"The reason Mr. Duncan is offended by these lost people being in church is that he is the one who has no burden for a lost world. In addition to that, his own statements before you indicate that he is prejudiced against those of other races and social standing--he thinks he is too good to associate with them and if he had his way he would not allow them in the church. Can a man like this bring a charge against another man about not being burdened for souls?"

Garth squirmed in his seat and started to speak. But I wasn't going to give him a chance. I rolled on.

"Most of the other accusations flow out of the matter of membership accountability. For years the First Baptist church has not held its membership accountable. As a result we have a very impure membership. In fact, most of the members are either inactive or non-resident. About fifty to sixty are active. It is our desire, mine and the leadership and active members of the church, that we begin to practice responsible church membership with the installation of a plan of formative and reformative church discipline. But it has been a very difficult matter to put such a plan into effect because of the opposition of Mr. Duncan and his group of inactive members."

He did speak up now with a red face and loud tone.

"We're not inactive. We're attending every Sunday!"

He had played right into my hands.

"Gentlemen, let me tell you how Mr. Duncan and his group attend our church. They never come to the preaching or prayer services. They refuse to attend the regular established Sunday School classes. Rather, he and his group have set up an unauthorized Sunday School class-- they walked right in without any church vote or authority, chose their own teacher, and have been meeting and advocating policies opposite that of the established vote and leadership of the church ever since."

The committee was scowling by now. Most of them being pastors couldn't cotton to such actions as that.

I wasn't finished.

"Several weeks ago when Mr. Duncan and his group didn't get their way in a church business meeting, they walked out yelling and screaming and requesting that we remove their names from the church roll and that they intended never to come back. This we did, convinced it might be the best thing that could happen at this point in the history of the church.

"But Mr. Duncan and his group decided they had acted hastily and he came around and wanted to be reinstated. He wanted to negotiate and compromise when that which was at stake was the truth and could not be negotiated or compromised. When he could not get his way, he began to throw his weight around and make all kinds of threats. They gave me a month to resign, and if I didn't they would get rid of me one way or another, whatever it took."

I did not want to speak longer than necessary to make my case, so I concluded.

"Gentlemen, I will be glad to elaborate on any of these matters or accusations, but I think I have said enough to present my case. I know I can trust you men to agree that there are insufficient grounds to declare me a heretic. I am an Evangelistic Baptist, and am proud of it, and will continue to be so whatever this committee or association does."

The chairman, Brother Jones, took control of the floor.

"Gentlemen, I think we have heard enough to make a decision. But just to be sure, let me ask Mr. Duncan several questions, and I expect him to answer so we all can hear."

Garth shifted in his chair and cleared his throat somewhat embarrassed.

"Mr. Duncan, did you or did you not with your group start an unauthorized Sunday School class in the First Baptist Church of Collegetown?"

He stuttered and stammered and then replied, "We had to if we were going to have any chance to regain control of our church."

"Mr. Duncan, did you or did you not ask for your name to be removed from the roll of the First Baptist Church of Collegetown?"

"Yes," he shouted, "but then I changed my mind and I think they should be willing to take me back."

"Mr. Duncan, did you or did you not give Brother Pointer an ultimatum that he resign by a certain date or you would someway see that he was removed?"

Garth's face turned red.

"Yes, but we had to do it or he'll stay forever and ruin the church."

"Mr. Duncan," the chairman asked with the Mr. getting more emphasis each time. "Do you have a problem with blacks and minority groups attending and joining First Baptist Church of Collegetown?"

"Well, they've got their own churches, haven't they?" he stated arrogantly.

"Mr. Duncan, do you or do you not know what a Calvinist is?"

Then the chairman added, "You had better be honest with this question, because if you say yes I will ask you for a definition."

Garth hung his head, and almost silently but still rebelliously stated, "Well, sort of."

"Speak up, Mr. Duncan. We can't hear you clearly," the chairman chided.

"I said, sort of."

Brother Jones said in response, "I'll take that as a negative answer. We can't recommend a man be brought before the whole local denominational body on heresy charges on a 'sort of' basis."

With these questions, the committee voted to recommend to the executive representatives at the next meeting that all accusations against Rev. Ira F. Pointer were unfounded.

Garth walked out as we were praying unwilling to face the group after their decision.

I hoped he had experienced some change of heart or mind about the coming ultimatum on Sunday, but I wouldn't have wanted to stake my life on it.

Give me God to help me, and I will split the world in halves, and shiver it till it shall be smaller than the dust of the threshing floor; ay, and if God be with me, this breath could blow whole worlds about, as the child bloweth a bubble. There is no saying what man can do when God is with him. Give God to a man, and he can do all things. Put God into a man's arm, and he may have only the jawbone of an ass to fight with, but he will lay the Philistines in heaps: put God into a man's hand, and he may have a giant to deal with, and nothing but a sling and a stone, but he will lodge the stone in the giant's brow before long; put God into a man's eye, and he will flash defiance on kings and princes; put God into a man's lip, and he will speak right honestly, though death should be the wages of his speech. There is no fear of a man who has God with him; he is all-sufficient, there is nothing beyond his power.

---C. H. Spurgeon

CHAPTER 37

LORD, WHAT WILL YOU HAVE US TO DO?

I will even make a way in the wilderness, and rivers in the desert.
Isaiah 43:19

Any hope that ultimatum Sunday was called off vanished with the passing of the next day, a Wednesday. Again, my phone rang continually with new information about the plans and actions of the opposition party.

I learned by means of these calls that their over-all strategy was to take over the Sunday morning services and force a vote on several key issues. They were determined to reinstate those we had voted out, to fire me as pastor, and to remove all the other officers of the church, especially the deacons.

To accomplish this they were calling all members and former members by telephone, and they were urging them to be present for such a forced business meeting. Further they weren't just inviting the members and formers members, but they were urging them to bring anyone they could round up regardless of who they were. They hoped such great numbers would give them not only the victory in the vote, but also a psychological edge. And since no one knew all the members, it wouldn't matter if some non-members were in the group, and maybe even voted.

Again, one caller informed me that they had several letters from Baptists high up in the denominational hierarchy who agreed with them and disagreed with us over the matter of Baptist polity, and those letters would be read at the Sunday service.

I couldn't believe such tactics could be used by anyone, including them, but with each call, and with a thorough quizzing of each caller, I finally became convinced this was their plan of action.

As we gathered for prayer meeting that evening, there was no one present except our group. I shared with them the plans of the opposition for the coming Sunday. During the course of prayer, someone raised the question with the Lord as they were praying, if He might have us leave and start a new church.   I had thought of that possibility, but had a strong conviction about church splits. I had heard all the jokes around school that this was the Baptist missions program to start new churches--the church split--and that if it weren't for splits, Evangelistic Baptists would never start a new church.

Most of the church splits I had known about had been over small and insignificant things.   Such mammoth questions dominated their motives, like where are we going to put the piano? Or what color are we going to paint the wall of the sanctuary? Or who will be the Sunday School director or teacher? Few were ever over doctrine.

Therefore, some people looked upon splits as always something evil and impossible if one were truly spiritual. Only selfish people who are unwilling to negotiate and compromise split as they are unable to work out their problems, was the attitude of the day.

Furthermore, to be the one who splits off carried even greater negative connotation. After all, if some leave us, then they have the problem. But if we leave them, that is a very humbling experience for you seem to have lost the battle, whatever it was over, and your opponent has won. Any good American is a poor loser. No good loser is truly a good American. We would rather die than appear to lose. Drag the other guy down with you, but don't go down alone. Better to have two losers, rather than to see one of the parties appear to win.

So goes the mentality we bear from our youth, it seems. And what would the enemy say if we were to leave and give them all the buildings, the funds, and documents? Would they not gloat in childish glee seeing our action as an admission they had won and we had lost?

And what if our new group never made it? What if it died? Wouldn't the enemy gloat again? And wouldn't the community even sit back and shake their heads at what fools we had been?

And would all our people go with us? Many of them had been reared in this church. They had been saved there. They had been baptized there. They had been married there. They had taught there and served there. They had invested a great amount of funds there. They had family members they would have to leave behind there. Would it be fair to ask them to leave, and would they leave even if we asked them?

Maybe it would be better just for me to leave. But would that not be saying that I was the issue, when I really was not? The truth of the Scripture was the issue. And if I left, I would leave the saints alone with the impure minority of Garth and his kind, and what would they do for spiritual life and growth?

I went home that night quite confused but willing to do whatever the Lord led me to do. I was ready to stay and fight for the truth, or I was ready to go and stand for the truth elsewhere where we could build a church with purity and godliness.

Several more phone calls that evening from my own people let me know I was not the only one confused and unsure of the future. Yet everyone I talked with was open to follow the Lord wherever He led us.

The only questions were, Lord, what will You have us to do? and how will we know when to do it? The hour of decision and reckoning was quickly approaching.

But a certain man named Ananias, with Sapphira, his wife sold a possession.

And kept back part of the price, his wife being privy to it, and brought a certain part and laid it at the apostles' feet.

But Peter said, Ananias, why hath Satan filled thine heart to lie to the Holy Spirit, and to keep back part of the price of the land?

While it remained, was it not thine own? And after it was sold, was it not in thine own power? Why has thou conceived this thing in thine heart? Thou hast not lied unto men, but unto God.

And Ananias hearing these words fell down and died; and great fear came on all them that heard these things.

And the young men arose, wound him up, and carried him out, and buried him.

And it was about the space of three hours after, when his wife, not knowing what was done, came in.

And Peter answered her, Tell me whether ye sold the land for so much? And she said, Yea, for so much.

Then Peter said unto her, How is it that ye have agreed together to tempt the Spirit of the Lord? Behold, the feet of them who have buried thy husband are at the door, and shall carry thee out.

Then fell she down straightway at his feet, and died; and the young men came in, and found her dead, and carrying her forth, buried her by her husband.

And great fear came upon all the church, and upon as many as heard these things.

---Acts 5:1-11

CHAPTER 38

IS THERE A SYSTEM OF DISCIPLINE IN THE BIBLE?

We ought to obey God, rather than men.
Acts 5 :29

Thursday evening found me with the deacons once again. They were buzzing with apprehension regarding the coming Sunday. As I conducted our study session, I made very little reference to it.

"Men, I realize we have not dealt with all verses which could be considered when thinking of church discipline. But we have dealt with enough that I think it is now time to review and put together what we have studied into some kind of plan or system."

I smiled and wanted to say, "We will have a system, but don't expect it to work this Sunday. But it would have worked if the church would have been employing it the past years instead of totally neglecting discipline."

Instead, I showed them my thoughts in the following study outline.

INTRODUCTION

The word discipline often has negative connotations. However, that shouldn't always be the case. Though the discipline responsibility of the church falls into positive discipline (formative discipline) and negative discipline (reformative discipline), they both should bear a positive influence on the church.

The positive discipline (formative) is the teaching and educating program of the church whereby all members, but especially the new members, are taught and trained in Christian doctrine and life.

The negative discipline (reformative) should not carry, however, any negative connotation either, for it is for the best of the church and every individual member. It should leave a positive impact on the church--the impact of purity and godliness.

The clear principles of discipline which we have gleaned from this study are as follows:

I   THERE EXIST SOME CLEAR DIVISIONS IN THE DISCIPLINE RESPONSIBILITY OF THE CHURCH

    1. There is the discipline of serious sin which has been committed by one whose attitude remains boldly unrepentant (I Corinthians 5:1-5).

    2. There is the discipline of the sin of one brother against another (Matthew 18:15-18).

    3. There is the discipline of the sin which has overtaken a brother and has left him sorrowful and crushed (Galatians 6:1).

    4. There is the discipline of one teaching false doctrine (I Timothy 6:3-5).

    5. There is the discipline of one not walking as a Christian should walk in his daily life (II Thessalonians 3:6: II Thessalonians 3:14-15).

I noted for them that this pretty well covers the spectrum of the categories of sin.

II THERE EXIST SOME CLEAR COMMON PRINCIPLES IN THE DISCIPLINE RESPONSIBILITY OF THE CHURCH

    1. The church is the final authority in the matter of discipline.

2. The leaders of the church are the agents to carry out the discipline program because they are the most spiritual of the membership of the church.

3. The Scripture is the authority regarding a standard whereby one is judged concerning his sin in practice or doctrine.

III THERE EXIST SOME CLEAR DIFFERENCES FROM CASE TO CASE IN THE DISCIPLINE RESPONSIBILITY OF THE CHURCH

1. In the matter of <u>one with serious sin and an unrepentant heart,</u> the action of the church is severe-- to turn such a one over to the devil for the destruction of the flesh that his spirit may be saved in the day of the Lord Jesus Christ.

2. In the matter of <u>one brother sinning against another,</u> the action of excommunication (treat him as a heathen or publican) by the church is necessary if the sinning brother refuses to listen to the church.

3. In the matter of <u>one who has sinned and is sorrowful and crushed by it,</u> there is to be restoration to Christ and the church by the spiritual members of the church in a spirit of meekness and humility.

4. In the matter of the <u>one guilty of false teaching,</u> the action of excommunication (withdraw thyself from him) must be enacted by the church.

5. In the matter of <u>one who refuses to live like a Christian,</u> the action of the church is again to be excommunication (withdrawal of fellowship), but the offender is not to be treated as a lost man but is to be admonished as a brother.

I noted that in all cases there is the possibility of repentance and restoration--that is hoped for in every case. Also I acknowledged that there is much more to be worked out from these principles, but at least these give some guidance for the church to proceed with their important responsibility of church purity.

IV THERE EXIST SOME CLEAR DANGERS TO BE AVOIDED IN THE DISCIPLINE RESPONSIBILITY OF THE CHURCH

Though these are not all spelled out clearly in Scripture, and though I had stated them previously, I felt it was necessary and helpful to state them again.

1. Pride--the work of discipline must be done with a humble heart.

2. Legalism--the work of discipline is not just a set of rules which are mechanically and coldly applied so we can say we have been faithful to the keeping of the rules.

3. Extremism--the work of discipline does not lead us to the place where we play Holy Spirit or God in one's life, whereby we want to make their decisions for them.

4. Undisciplined discipline--the work of discipline must be structured and clearly principled, and the principles must be applied fairly and consistently in each case and from one case to another.

5. Arbitrariness--the work of discipline must be based on Scripture not only as to how it is to be done, but also concerning matters for which one is to be disciplined, and not on matters of someone or several persons' arbitrary choice.

6. Supremacy--the work of discipline must not be seen to be the supreme and only work of the church, but

rather it is part of the necessary work the church is engaged in.

7. <u>Asceticism</u>--the work of discipline must never be seen as an end and goal unto itself or as a means which by itself can produce spirituality and growth.

We could have stayed a long time this Thursday evening and discussed these principles. But I had promised myself at the beginning of the study that we would try to get the men home at a fairly decent hour.

But we could not avoid several questions, although I'm not sure we answered them.

Why have these truths been lost to the church?

How long has it been since any of us heard a sermon on these verses or this subject, not counting the months Brother Ira has been here?

How can these principles ever be re-established in a church like ours?

Can you imagine the joy of starting a new church and establishing the matter of purity from the beginning?

Perhaps the last two questions were the most important and clearly related to one another. But then, anything of the nature of the last question was in God's hands.

When the wicked, even mine enemies and my foes
    came upon me to eat my flesh,
They stumbled and fell.

Though an host should encamp against me
    my heart shall not fear:
Though war should rise against me,
    in this will I be confident.
And now shall mine head be lifted up above mine enemies
    round about me.

---*Psalms 27:2-3, 6*

I said unto the Lord,
    Thou art my God;
    Hear the voice of my supplication, O, Lord.
O God, the Lord, the strength of my salvation;
    Thou has covered my head in the day of battle.

---*Psalms 140:6-7*

CHAPTER 39

WHO CALLS THE SHOTS
FOR ETERNITY?

Thou couldest have no power against me,
except it were given thee from above...
John 19:11

The tension was building as we moved closer to Sunday. I sensed it in our people. I sensed it in Terry's attitude. I sensed it in my own life. The opposition was doing all it could to tighten the screws on us.

Even Garth made one final run at me as he showed up in my office on Friday morning. All pretense in attitude and speech was gone. This day he was what he was.

"Well, preacher, it won't be long now. Have you got another place to go?" he said with a joyful smile.

"Garth, haven't you got better things to do today than come around and bother people who are trying to work?"

"Listen, preacher!" he shot back. "I've got a deal to make with you, if only you're bright enough to listen."

"I have no desire to hear it!"

"Don't you realize that we have the people and the commitment to do anything we want this Sunday?"

"Only if God wills!" I reminded him. "You can do nothing outside of God's will"

"Well, God must be willing then, because we can do whatever we want with you, the church and the deacons," he bragged.

"Garth, the day will come when you will regret what you are planning to do this Sunday. It may be before Sunday. It may be after next Sunday. It may be sickness. It may be death. It may be sorrow of the deepest kind. I don't know all of God's ways. But I know this--someday, somewhere, somehow, you will have to pay for what you are doing. The Bible is clear on that, but I don't hardly expect you to believe or understand that, because you don't seem to believe or

understand anything else the Bible has to say. Now, please
let me get some work done."

"Oh, you enjoy saying that, don't you preacher?" he
challenged.

"No, I don't enjoy saying that. And I won't rejoice
when the judgment of God falls on you. And if I am there, I
will love you and seek to help you. But I must warn you
that you can be sure your sins will find you out. A man
reaps what he sows, and you are sowing some powerfully
strong sin of the worst kind."

"Well, preacher, I was going to tell you we would let
you stay in the parsonage for a month, if you cooperated and
resigned before we have to vote you out Sunday. Now,
after we've voted, you've got twenty-four hours to get out
of our parsonage, or we will throw you out."

"And what if I ask the law to deal with you for your
actions?" I asked.

"Oh, some of our boys, as you found out one night a
few weeks ago, have ways of convincing you to go. Give
them a week and you'll go on your own."

I was getting a little upset with him by now. I knew if
he said much more, I would deck him. So I figured it was
time to get rid of him in the only way I could.

"Garth, before you go, let me read to you from several
Scripture passages, and I want to pray for you."

That was all he needed to excuse himself and leave
almost immediately.

His parting remark was frightening.

"You can read your Bible, and you can pray all you
want, but there's nothing anyone can do to help you--not
your deacons, not your little group of members, not your
group of drop-outs, not even God Himself. We're calling
the shots now."

My reply stung sharply.

"Garth, you may think now you are calling the shots
Sunday, and you may even think on Sunday night that you
called the shots for that day also. But I'll guarantee you that
God calls the shots each day whatever blind unspiritual
mortals may think. And remember, He calls the shots for
eternity."

CHAPTER 40

HOW DO YOU PURIFY
AN IMPURE CHURCH?

Behold, the Lord's hand is not shortened that it cannot save,
neither his ear heavy, that it cannot hear.
Isaiah 59:1

Time was not just dragging by the time Saturday evening arrived--it seemed to have stopped. I thought about calling off the Saturday evening deacons' meeting, but then decided against it. The time together would allow us to encourage one another as well as to pray together. I must admit that I hadn't planned that our last study on discipline would correspond with ultimatum Sunday eve, but in God's providence it did.

We began with a rather extended season of prayer--not only for God to guide us, but that He might change the heart of the enemy, especially Garth Duncan. If the grace of God is for sinners, then Garth Duncan was a clear candidate.

We then moved into the study as I reminded them of our Thursday evening discussion. Then I presented a plan to implement a program of discipline in a church.

1. Obviously, it is easiest to keep a church pure if Biblical principles of discipline are installed from the beginning of the church's history and they are upheld in the passing of the years.

2. Obviously, again, many of the churches of our day have not done this, and as a result today have a very impure membership of uncommitted, unconcerned, inactive, uninvolved and even some non-resident members. How does one bring purity to such a church as this? Let me state some principles to follow when attempting to lead

such a church back to purity and responsible
membership.

a. Move slowly being sure you have an understanding
    of the principles of church discipline and a plan to
    implement them.

    (This had been part of our problem at First Baptist
    Church. The sleeping giant of the inactive member-
    ship woke up before we had time to set forth the
    principles and lay a plan.)

b. The plan to implement the principles of church
    discipline should include the following:

    A thorough listing of all the membership of the
        church, active and inactive and non-resident,
        along with their addresses and other available
        information concerning their relationship to the
        church.

    An initial attempt to contact each resident member in
        person and each non-resident member by letter to
        determine their spiritual standing at the present
        hour, and their intents for the future. Such
        contact could be an evangelistic contact, if such
        members have never been saved, or a re-
        enlistment contact if they are saved but inactive.
        It is admitted that it is not always easy to
        distinguish the two, but, nonetheless, the visit
        should be made by trained persons who are
        ready to carry the visit in the direction of the
        individual's need.

    A continuing attempt to contact and minister to these
        whose names are on the roll of the church,
        urging the inactive members to return to the
        church, dealing with evangelistic needs as the
        visitation unfolds, and urging the non-resident
        members to become active in the place where

they live. Do not be surprised if all kinds of
responses greet you in this phase of the task.
Some will appreciate the contact and effort to
restore them, while others will not. All must be
done in love and humility regardless of the
response of the people.

<u>A solid and continual exposition of the Word of God</u>
book by book, presenting the Biblical teaching
on all facets of the truth as it is found in the
Scriptures. By this means those attending will be
grounded in all aspects of the faith once delivered
to the saints, including the clear definition and
characteristics of true salvation. They will learn
also to recognize its results and accompaniments
in an individual's life. Do not be surprised if this
Biblical preaching is not received by all. For
some it will not be exciting or sensational
enough. That is not to say the preacher is
to set forth the truth in some dead and
uninteresting manner, but that many, being
unsaved, do not have a heart to hear and
understand the truth. One of the fruits of such
preaching will be an understanding of the need of
purity in the church as the hearers see what true
salvation is and then compare it with what the
church has been advocating in its doctrine and
practice.

<u>A teaching on the passages on church discipline</u>, not
necessarily all at once, but separately. This is
best done as one preaches through the individual
books of the Bible and deals with each passage in
its specific context. Obviously, it will take a
preacher some time to preach through all the
Bible, especially the New Testament in reference
to this subject. Therefore, when it is deemed that
the church has a sufficient capability to grasp the
truth of the passages, a series on the subject
would not be out of order. If such a series is set

forth, it is best to do it at a time when the most
spiritual people of the congregation are present,
perhaps to the leadership of the church or on a
Wednesday evening for those attending the
prayer service.

A study of the practice and history of church
discipline by the local church where one is
working and also of the denomination. Most
Baptist churches have records in their earlier
history of the practice of discipline. Also,
Baptists of history had clear principles and
undeniably practiced church discipline in the
past. That is not to say they always did it
correctly, but it cannot be denied that church
purity was a concern of earlier Baptists.
One of the finest documents of Baptist
history concerning the practice of discipline
is A Summary of Church Discipline which
was set forth by the the Baptist Association
in Charleston, South Carolina.[1]

A setting forth of the principles of church discipline
to the leadership of the church and to the church
itself. This should be followed by the church, if
it is congregationally ruled, accepting these
principles as those to be followed in the practice
of discipline in the church. If the church is elder
ruled, then the elders accept the principles. Such
principles should be clear and comprehensive and
with a certain fullness so that there will be no
question or doubt about what is to be done when
occasions of discipline arise. Obviously then the
people are to be educated as to the principles
adopted.

The practice of discipline begins when all the above
is in order. That is, when the church has clear
understanding of how to do it, and when the
people who are inactive and non-resident have

been dealt with for a period of time and given time to amend their ways, then the principles begin to be put into effect. It is important to keep those needing correction informed as to each step of this part of the discipline as it unfolds. A letter or two of information as to what the church is doing and the necessity to become active again is needful. Another letter of warning of the consequences if one does not become active once again is also essential. Remember, this follows a period of personal contact. When the appointed time has arrived, those who have not responded are dealt with in the manner prescribed in the program set up by the church. Some churches have moved those making no response to an inactive roll, and then give such a person another period of time to be restored to the active roll. If there is no response during the allotted time, then the person is dropped from the roll.

c. Don't be surprised at any response you might get to the work of church discipline.

The sleeping giant may wake up and ruin the whole plan. Then one can only cast himself and the church on the Lord, especially if the sleeping giant is a majority.

The majority of the church could accept the preaching and teaching of the Word and the need of discipline, and then two possibilities could follow.

1) a disagreeable minority might stay for awhile and fight but then leave when seeing the impossibility of the task of overthrowing the truth and the work of discipline.

2) a disagreeable minority might take up the fight and be so militant and uncontrollable

> that the majority, unless God clearly
> intervenes, will have to leave in order to
> have peace and establish a pure church.

We lingered at the end of our study for another season in prayer due to the concern on our hearts for tomorrow. Garth Duncan was heavy on our hearts. A special presence of the Lord was upon us. People wept in brokenness and concern. We left uncertain of what events would break upon us the next day, but certain of His sovereignty over them and willing to receive whatever He sent to us.

---

[1]James Leo Garrett, Jr., *Baptist Church Discipline* (Nashville: Broadman Press, 1962).

CHAPTER 41

WHAT DOES HE WANT AT THE MIDNIGHT HOUR?

I who speak in righteousness, am mighty to save.
Isaiah 63:1

It was 10:30 by the time I got home Saturday evening.
And shortly thereafter I crawled into bed--exhausted, but
even then not sure I could sleep in light of the concern for
tomorrow. But I conked out immediately into a deep sleep--
until the phone rang.

My mind was as fuzzy as a boxer who had just hit the
canvas as I picked up the phone.

"Hello!" I offered as best I could into the phone.

"Ira, this is Todd. I've got to see you tonight--right
away. It's important!"

"Todd, it's past eleven!" I protested as I squinted in the
darkness at my watch.

Todd was my best friend in college. He professed faith
in Christ as a teenager, and then surrendered to preach. For
awhile after that he was a sensational but shallow preacher as
well as a selfish and frivolous individual. He was my room
mate in college and just about drove me nuts with his life-
style of self-indulgence and pride.

Then one day he realized he had never been saved, and
God had truly changed his life. He then followed me as
pastor at my first church, the Lime Creek Baptist Church. I
had seen him grow in such evident maturity, but every once
in awhile he showed some of the old Todd, and I was sure
this was one of those times.

"Believe me, Ira. I've got to see you. I'll be there in
forty minutes," he rattled. And with that he hung up.

I could have wrung his neck. What in the world could
be so important that he had to see me on Saturday night at
the midnight hour when I was exhausted and facing the
biggest day of my life in just a few hours? I felt towards

him like I had before he was saved, when he was cutting up and acting the part of the an empty-headed child.

I waited in the living room stewing and planning to straighten him out once and for all when he arrived.

Then his car pulled into my driveway. I turned the porch light on and squinted out between the curtains. Someone was with him--one of his girl friends, maybe? That's all I need at this hour. Todd with girl-friend trouble.

It became obvious as they walked towards the porch that it was a man. But who? When they stepped into the light and I could recognize them both, I couldn't believe the identity of the other party with him.

It was Garth--Garth Duncan! What in the world was he doing with Todd?

As I opened the door and Todd stepped through, it was at first nothing but silence. Then Todd spoke and was as serious as I had ever known him to be.

"Ira, Garth has something he wants to tell you."

Garth broke into tears.

Then he spoke.

"Pastor, God saved me tonight. Can you ever forgive me for all the things I've done to hurt you?"

Then I began to cry. I assured him that as God's grace had forgiven him, so I had forgiven him also. We hugged one another, while Todd stood by emitting "Amens" and "Praise the Lords."

When the initial shock had settled, Garth shared with me how he had been under conviction for several weeks, but didn't know it. The conviction became heavier the closer we got to ultimatum Sunday. That's why he came by my office on Friday--he was hurting so badly. Yet all the time he had no idea the misery was because God was speaking to him.

Then this Saturday evening he was visiting his son and his family forty miles outside of Collegetown. His son's church was in revival, and Todd was the preacher. He went mainly because he found out Todd was a close friend of mine and thought he might find out some final dirt on me after the service.

But God spoke to him as Todd delivered the Word and utterly broke him in half. On the way out as he was shaking hands with Todd, he broke down crying and pled for someone to show him how to be saved. Todd took him aside, talked with him, and led him to the Lord.

In the further unburdening of his heart he told Todd of his actions against me. Todd knew someone was leading the opposition against me, but he had no idea that someone was in the service as he preached that night. He spoke on sin finding one out, just as I had warned Garth on Friday.

After he had shared with Todd what he had done against me, Garth insisted that they come to see me right away, which they did. Now he wanted to undo all the wrong he had stirred against me. He wanted to know how to go about it.

I had to admit that this was quite a problem. How do you quiet down a hornet's nest which you have just stirred up? How does one put out a fire which has been fed with hundreds of gallons of gasoline? How do you stop a speeding train in an instant?

We went to our knees in prayer, knowing God must direct us. Then I suggested that he call the two most influential men of the group he led and share with them what had happened and tell them the meeting against us was called off.

He picked up the phone rather gingerly almost as if he was frightened. I wondered why so many times it is easier to be bold for sinful practices than for godly actions.

He got the same answer from both men. He was to them as one who was joking. They didn't believe he could possibly mean it. They laughed and hung up on him thinking he was playing games with them.

"There's only one thing to do!" he finally concluded. "I must go in the morning and speak to the whole group and seek to disburse them. Yet I realize that what I have done is liable to get us both killed! They are really stirred up, thanks to my sin and godlessness."

The kings of the earth stood up, and the rulers were gathered together against the Lord, and against His Christ. For of a truth against the holy servant Jesus, whom Thou hast anointed, both Herod and Pontius Pilate, with the Gentiles, and the people of Israel were gathered together, for to do whatsoever Thy hand and Thy counsel determined before to be done.

---Acts 4:26-28

The supreme example of the controlling, directing influence which God exerts upon the wicked, is the Cross of Christ with all its attendant circumstances. If ever the superintending providence of God was witnessed, it was there. From all eternity God had predestined every detail of that event of all events. Nothing was left to chance or the caprice of man. God had decreed when and where and how His blessed Son was to die....Not a thing occured except as God had ordained, and all that He had ordained took place exactly as He purposed.

---Arthur W. Pink

CHAPTER 42

CAN IT REALLY BE OVER?

There is no wisdom, nor understanding,
nor counsel against the Lord.
Proverbs 21:30

Understandably, I hardly slept the remainder of the night. My emotions were so scrambled by now. I had gone from one whose heart had been crushed to the lowest level to a height of rejoicing I had never known before in all my Christian life. Yet at the same time my heart was still heavy with the uncertainty of the morning upon us.

As we finally gathered for the Sunday School hour, it was obvious something unusual was going to take place at First Baptist Church that day. But who knew what the outcome would be.

Garth's group over-ran their Sunday School area, and it was to be assumed more would follow at the eleven o'clock hour. And sure enough, at about 10:40 the crowd began to gather into the sanctuary and the building began to buzz.

The faithful numbered their usual sixty or so. Garth's group swelled into the hundreds, and there were so many of them I didn't know and hadn't even seen before. And then there was Dink's group of about twenty-five again.

Garth had tried to address the Sunday School class, but had been flatly rejected. It was obvious that the freight train was going to be hard to stop at this point.

When we finally started the service, the number in the building must have been about five hundred. Maybe they would chicken out and not make any disturbance, especially without Garth's leadership. The prelude and call to worship and first song passed without any problem or interference.

It was when I got up to make a few announcements that the chaos broke loose. The new leader, the heir to Garth's mantle, demanded he be given the floor. I called to his attention that we were not in a business session of the church, but were in a worship service. But he would not listen.

Garth then rose to speak. They listened, at least for awhile.

"I want to publicly confess my sin against God and this church and my pastor, Brother Ira. I was as a wild man-- even like the apostle Paul on the road to Damascus. I was persecuting the church and the people of God in the name of God, thinking all the time I was doing His service. I also falsely influenced many of you. But last night God arrested me and saved me. He showed me my lostness and the sin of what I had been doing against Him and this man of God and this church. I have asked him to forgive me and he has. I have asked God to forgive me and He has. Now I ask you to forgive me for lying to you and misleading you. I ask you to cease all harassment of this man and this church, return to your homes, and consider the gravity of the rebellious act you have come here to perform. Please, go now! Please!"

For a few moments there was silence throughout the building. I was reminded of the probable silence which followed for a few moments when Pilate proclaimed Christ's innocence--that is until the religious leaders began to stir the crowd once again.

And the same thing happened here. The men Garth had enlisted to be his chief accomplices began to stir the crowd.

"We will have a meeting! We will take a vote!" they all began to cry.

What could the faithful sixty do? The godly are always at a disadvantage, humanly speaking, in such a meeting. They have inhibitions and rules by which they live, while the ungodly do not.

I was a little concerned about Dink's group. His method, and I am sure the method of those with him, had always been to solve problems by the skill of guns and knives. I could see they were getting more and more upset by the minute. He had been the kind of guy who acted and spoke later, if there was anyone left to speak to.

One of the leaders began to yell above the roar of the crowd, as he waved a piece of paper.

"We have letters from the highest officials of our denomination stating this pastor is out of order."

And then the crowd boomed even louder, "We will have a meeting! We will have a meeting! We will have a meeting!"

I tried to speak several times, but was drowned at each attempt. Garth tried to speak, but he was given the same treatment.

Then the scene became even more explosive as one of the opposition yelled, "And when you leave, take that scum of society with you. We don't want their kind in our church!"

He not only insulted Dink and his friends, but he also made a fist and shook it at them.

With that insult and action I turned and started towards the door at the front which led out of the sanctuary, and immediately the spiritual sixty followed me out. Then as I looked around when in the hall, here came Dink and his friends behind us also. And Garth was with us too!

I went straight to my study, loaded my books up in some boxes, and with the help of several others carried them to several cars. Then Terry and I went home, as did the others.

We shed some tears as we left, thinking of what could have been, but, honestly, we were relieved that it was all over.

Then we realized that God had a greater purpose. If this was what it took to bring Garth Duncan to Christ, it was worth it all. It had cost Christ far more to save us and him.

I slept like a baby for several hours that afternoon not even thinking of tomorrow, let alone of Sunday evening.

It was over, and I had no desire for these moments to even think about the future.

But the Lord said unto me, Say not, I am a child; for thou shalt go to all that I shall I send thee, and whatsoever I command thee thou shalt speak.

Be not afraid of their faces; for I am with thee to deliver thee, saith the Lord.

---Jeremiah 1:7-8

The Lord is my helper, and I will not fear what man shall do unto me.
---Hebrews 13:6

The messenger of the Lord should never be affected by those to whom he delivers his message; he should be above them, while at the same time he takes the humble place of a servant. His language should be, 'But with me, it is a very small matter that I should be judged of you or of man's judgment'.
--C. H. Mackintosh

CHAPTER 43

WHAT ARE WE GOING TO DO TONIGHT?

*Said I not unto thee, that if thou wouldest believe,
thou shouldest see the glory of God?*
John 11:40

It had been a long time since I slept on Sunday afternoon and then awakened with no place to go that evening. Particularly, I was glad not to have to go back to First Baptist Church.

Terry was reading when I walked out of the bedroom into the living room.

"Well, have you got your sermon for tonight?" she asked kiddingly, I thought.

I laughed and offered some statement about going to preach on the stink in the sanctuary.

"You've got about an hour to decide what you're speaking on tonight," she said with a straight face.

"What are you talking about?" I asked.

"We're meeting tonight at Conrad Spratt's house. The deacons have notified everyone of the service--even Dink and his friends. They want to talk about starting a new church."

I thought maybe a new church might come out of all of this eventually, but not quite this soon. And I wasn't sure I was the one to start it. I got my Bible and began to search for a passage so I could at least give a devotional.

As we gathered that evening, it was a subdued and somber crowd--at least compared to what they usually were. Everyone was still in shock over the events of the morning, and, no doubt, unsure about the future. Almost everyone was there, including Dink and a few (not all) of his friends. And Garth and his family were there also. We were quite a group packed into Conrad Spratt's family room, everyone sitting somewhere, even some on the floor.

I spoke that night on Philippians 3:13-14:

> *13) Brethren, I count not myself to have apprehended; but this one thing I do, forgetting those things which are behind, and reaching forth unto those things which are before,*
> *14) I press toward the mark for the prize of the high calling of God in Christ Jesus.*

At the end of the message, we discussed the possibility of starting a new church. All were in favor of it--not one person dissented. We agreed, then, that this was what God would have us to do.

We ended the evening by singing our favorite song.

Amazing grace, how sweet the sound,
That saved a wretch like me.
I once was lost, but now am found.
Was blind, but now I see.

No one sang as freely and fervently as Garth Duncan. Tears streamed down his cheeks, and then the rest of us began to cry also.

But the verse which meant the most to the majority of us this night was the following:

Through many dangers, toils, and snares
We have already come.
'Twas grace that brought us safe thus far,
And grace will lead us home.

The greatest part of the evening was that the tension was gone. We could meet in peace. And we had a plan for the planting and maintaining of a pure church.

Several matters of immediate concern were resting before us. We would have to find a place to meet as a church--but we were confident He would guide us. Terry and I would have to find a place to live--but He could take care of that also. We would have to have a constitution and by-laws and a doctrinal statement.

Most of our doctrine was settled. But there was one area I had come to debate in my own mind which would be important in the life of the new church. What kind of government should our church have--congregational rule or elder rule?

I had seen some of the problems in a congregational ruled church in the last few weeks. But I was also aware of some of the problems which could arise in an elder ruled church. I suppose any form of church government would never work unless those involved in it were spiritual and godly in their lives.

The real question was, what form of government does the New Testament teach? Further, what form of government have Baptists practiced through their history?

Perhaps that could be my next theological search!

It looks like my study on eschatology will have to wait a little longer.